Merrick needs Alpin to stay away from him. Alpin wants the exact opposite.

Merrick only has a few people in his life, and he's fine with that. Being turned into a dragon shifter and vampire hybrid forcefully made him push away all vampires, but he can't push away Alpin, no matter how hard he tries to.

Alpin won't take no for an answer. He wants Merrick, and he always gets what he wants. Maybe it's because he's the youngest and more recent vampire in his family, or maybe it's because he's adorable and isn't afraid of using his pretty face. It always works.

But not this time.

Merrick is too good at resisting Alpin's charms, or maybe not. The last thing both Merrick and Alpin need is more complications, yet they can't stay away from each other. The dragon clan is plotting, though, and they find unlikely allies who know every weak spot the pack has.

And they're getting ready to attack.

Conflicting Fangs
Copyright © 2023 Catherine Lievens
ISBN: 978-1-4874-3778-7
Cover art by Angela Waters

Published by eXtasy Books Inc

Look for us online at:
www.eXtasybooks.com

CONFLICTING FANGS
LIFE WITH FANGS 10

BY

CATHERINE LIEVENS

CHAPTER ONE

For the first time since he could remember, Merrick wasn't looking forward to going to the club.

It had been his safe place after he and Arlen had left the clan. It was the one place where they could be whoever they wanted and didn't have to follow orders they disagreed with. It had taken them a lot of courage and money to start the club, but they had, and Merrick had been proud of it.

And now, it was nothing more than a bunch of burned-up walls and broken furniture.

He'd known that, of course. He'd already been here after the fire, so he knew what state everything was in and what to expect. That didn't make it any easier. The clan had taken the club away from him like they'd taken many other things. Merrick wanted nothing more than to go there, ravage every single property the clan owned, and leave them in a bunch of ashes, but he knew better. The clan was stronger, and they wouldn't hesitate to take him down if he even tried getting close to one of their properties.

So instead, he was left seething and snapping at the people helping him and Arlen. It wasn't right, but he didn't know how else to deal with the anger and pain. He needed to keep everyone away so he wouldn't lash out, which wasn't easy when they seemed intent on making him part of their family.

Merrick wasn't sure he'd ever understand those wolf shifters.

He might be a shifter like them, but that was all they had in common. Why were they so intent on him being one of them? It probably was because of Arlen. Arlen was dating a vampire—and Merrick had made sure his friend knew what he thought of that—and that vampire was somehow related to the pack. They'd pulled Arlen in, and Arlen had pulled Merrick right along because why not?

Merrick had a whole list of why it was a bad idea, but as he looked around the burned husk of what had once been his club, he thought that maybe it *wasn't* such a bad thing. He couldn't say he enjoyed spending time with so many people he barely knew, but he couldn't deny the pack had been there to help him and Arlen. It would take a while before they could set things right, but they were cleaning up the club, ensuring everything was in as good a state as possible so Arlen and Merrick could start rebuilding.

Because that was what they were planning. They wouldn't let the clan win. Merrick would rather die.

"You know, people are going to think you'll eat them if you stare at them that way," a soft voice said from beside Merrick.

Merrick took a deep breath. He needed all the patience he could find to deal with Alpin. Otherwise, he might slam him against the nearest wall, which was probably what Alpin was aiming for. Merrick wasn't sure if he'd do it to hurt Alpin or to fuck him, but he wasn't planning to find out.

He turned to look at the vampire. No one should be so pretty, especially when it came with the kind of personality Alpin had. He looked like an angel, with his blond curls, wide blue eyes, the rosiness of his cheeks, and his dimples, but he was anything but. If anything, he was a demon in disguise, and for some reason, he seemed intent on making Merrick's life hell.

"Come on. I'm sure you can give me a smile," Alpin prodded, stepping closer. He put a hand on Merrick's arm, and the gesture was anything but casual.

He was always touching Merrick, and Merrick wasn't sure

whether he liked it or not. His first instinct was to tell Alpin to fuck off, but he needed the vampires' help. He also wasn't sure he wanted Alpin to fuck off. He knew better than to get involved, because that way lay madness, but it was tempting, especially when Alpin made it clear he'd be on board with it.

"What do you want?" Merrick asked with a grunt.

Alpin's smile widened. "For you to smile at me."

Merrick could see a glimpse of his fangs, but he was starting to get used to being around vampires. He was pretty sure that what Alpin actually wanted was for him to show him his own fangs, but it wasn't going to happen. There was a reason Merrick never smiled.

It was the fangs.

"Don't you have better things to do?" Merrick asked.

"You mean better than asking you to smile for me? Nope."

Merrick pointedly looked around the room. "Are you sure?"

Anyone else would have left in a hurry, but not Alpin. Never him. He wasn't cowed by Merrick's bad mood. He wasn't intimidated or afraid, and that meant that Merrick had no idea how to deal with him. Most people ran away once they realized how grumpy Merrick was. Alpin, on the other hand, seemed to take it as a personal challenge. Merrick wouldn't have been surprised if Alpin truly just wanted him to smile.

He still wouldn't give him the satisfaction.

Alpin grinned and tapped a fingertip against his chin. "You know what I believe would make you smile?"

"I don't care." Merrick was kind of afraid to find out.

His words didn't stop Alpin. They never did.

"We should sleep together."

Merrick almost groaned, but he wouldn't give Alpin the satisfaction. "I believe I've already said no to that offer. Several times." Merrick looked around, hoping to find an escape, but everyone else was busy. He could start working, but he had no doubt that Alpin would follow him and continue talking to him, which he was trying to avoid.

"I'm a good lover," Alpin insisted. "I'm generous, and I'd make sure you're happy with what we do."

Merrick told himself that taking Alpin up on his offer would be a bad idea all around, but it was hard to convince himself of that. His dragon had taken a liking to Alpin because of course he had, and every time Alpin offered for them to have sex, the dragon sat up in the back of Merrick's mind and agreed. Thankfully, Merrick had control over that part of himself, but the problem was that his human part wanted Alpin as much as the dragon. He'd never admit it to anyone, not even Arlen, but he looked forward to the distraction Alpin provided, at least most of the time.

The rest of the time, he found Alpin incredibly frustrating.

He huffed, hoping Alpin would get the message that he was annoyed with him and needed to leave him alone.

Alpin did no such thing.

He bounced on the balls of his feet. "Think about it," he said.

"I have, and my answer is no." Merrick leaned down to pick up a broken chair. He'd have to throw it away, but then, he and Arlen would have to throw away most of the things in the club. It was a disaster, and he didn't know where to start.

"You realize that the more you say no, the more you make me want you, right?"

"I do, which makes me wonder if you realize just how predatory your behavior is."

Alpin's eyes widened, and he took a step back as if Merrick had hit him. "I'm sorry?"

"You're like one of those guys in bad nineties movies. When someone says no to you, you take it as a challenge instead of leaving them alone. If I wanted you, I'd say yes. I don't want you, and no is a full answer. Also, stop asking me to smile for you."

Alpin looked hurt, and while Merrick was sorry he'd made the vampire feel that way, maybe it wasn't a bad thing. Alpin needed to understand that not everyone was okay with what he did. Even though it was annoying, Merrick didn't actually mind, but what if Alpin had been trying to seduce someone else? For some reason, the thought of Alpin wanting someone else made Merrick's chest feel tight, but he decided he couldn't focus on that.

"I am *not* a predator," Alpin snapped, the smile finally gone from his lips.

"Could have fooled me."

"Why are you like this?"

"I don't know. Why are you like that?"

"I hate you."

"Good, because I don't like you."

Alpin glared before stomping away, leaving Merrick where he was and betraying how young he was. Merrick told himself it was a good thing and that he didn't want to spend any length of time with Alpin, but something in all of this made him feel bad.

He shook himself. How it made him feel didn't matter. He had work to do, and he needed to do it. The further away Alpin was from him, the better it would be for both of them.

Alpin stomped away from Merrick, angrier than he'd been in a long time. How dare Merrick tell him he was a predator?

Alpin huffed. He supposed he was, actually. He was a vampire, and it was their nature to be predators. But the same could be said about Merrick. The man wasn't just a dragon shifter. He was a vampire, just like Alpin, so maybe he should climb off his high horse and give Alpin a break.

But Alpin couldn't fool himself. Merrick hadn't been talking about drinking blood. He'd been talking about the way Alpin had been going after him, and Alpin couldn't deny he came on a bit strong sometimes. It wasn't that he couldn't take no for an answer. When he truly believed the people he was trying to seduce didn't want him, he took a step back and left them alone. None of them had been as interesting and fun to poke at as Merrick, though. That, along with Merrick's constant rejections, was part of why Alpin was so interested in him, but he doubted Merrick could see that.

Maybe Alpin should put some distance between them.

No matter how handsome he found Merrick, how fun it was to poke at him, the dragon was going through a lot. He'd almost lost the club, and even though some of the building was still l standing, it would take a lot of work and money to get it back to its former glory. All of that was because of the clan Merrick and Arlen had left behind, and it couldn't be easy for them to wrap their minds around the fact that people who were supposed to be family had done this to them.

Alpin didn't know what he'd do without his family. They were his world, and he'd do pretty much anything for them. That was why he was here, cleaning up the club even though he couldn't remember the last time he'd held a broom. This was important to Mallory, and Mallory was important to Alpin.

Maybe he should leave Merrick alone. The poor man was already dealing with enough, and Alpin would be the first to admit he was a lot to deal with. Most people who knew him were used to him, but Merrick wasn't. It might be good for Alpin to keep his distance.

Even though he really didn't want to.

What he wanted was to get into Merrick's pants. He wasn't sure why he was obsessed with the man, except maybe that it had to do with the fact that Merrick was both a dragon shifter and a vampire. Alpin was fascinated by that, and he wanted to find out how different it made Merrick from him, the other vampires, and his family. Could he breathe fire in his human form? Did he have fangs when he was a dragon? He certainly did in his human form, and while Alpin had never been much into biting when it came to sex, he couldn't deny he was curious.

But if he wanted to find out, he'd have to convince Merrick to give him a chance, and he wasn't sure how to do that. He'd tried being his seducing self, but Merrick hadn't fallen for it. If anything, he seemed to be pushing Alpin away harder, which wouldn't do.

So, how was Alpin supposed to get what he wanted?

"What have you done to him?" Mallory asked.

He was picking up trash in the corner, or at least, he had been. Right now, he was staring at Alpin, gloves on his hands, a trash bag clutched in one of them.

"Who said I did anything?" Alpin asked.

Mallory arched a brow. "Don't play innocent with me. I've known you since you became a vampire."

Alpin crossed his arms over his chest. "So you know I'm perfectly innocent."

Mallory laughed. "No one with eyes to watch you would think you're innocent." His expression turned more serious. "What did you do? I love you, and I always will, but we both know that when you get fixated on someone, you don't rest until you get what you want from them."

"Then you shouldn't be worried. I'll be fine as soon as I get Merrick."

"I'm not sure that will work. Merrick won't give in."

And Alpin wouldn't give up. It seemed they were at an impasse.

The thing was, Alpin wasn't about to change for a grumpy dragon vampire. But he realized that some people thought he was too much. He didn't want to marry Merrick. He just wanted to have fun with him in bed, or against a wall, or anywhere, really. Once the sex was over, Alpin would be able to move on, and he'd leave Merrick alone like Merrick wanted.

Maybe he should be honest about that. Maybe Merrick would give in if it meant Alpin would stay away from him after.

Mallory sighed. "Look, I know you don't mean any harm, but I think you should leave Merrick alone."

"Because you don't trust me with him?"

"I'd trust you with anything, including my life and Arlen's. But some people aren't going to want you, and you need to accept that. Merrick has a lot going on in his life, and he doesn't need you to make it worse."

A pang of *something* made Alpin's chest feel tight. "Maybe he needs a distraction."

"Maybe. He should be the one deciding that, though. What is it about him that's pushing you to be like this?"

Alpin shrugged. "I don't know. I just find him interesting." He didn't know why he wanted to get under Merrick's skin so badly, but he wasn't done trying. Maybe seducing Merrick so openly wasn't working, but that just meant he'd have to find another way. He was stubborn enough that he didn't care how long it would take him, but maybe Merrick hadn't realized that yet.

"I just hope you know what you're doing," Mallory said.

"I never do, but things always end up fine."

"If you say so. Just remember everything Merrick is dealing with, okay? It's not just the club. It's also the clan that's coming for them, plus losing their home."

Because Merrick and Arlen had been living above the club.

The same pang of emotion that had squeezed up Alpin's chest earlier came back. He couldn't even imagine how he'd feel if he lost his home. He didn't *want* to think about it. He didn't understand how Merrick and Arlen were still standing, but he supposed it had a lot to do with the fact that they had people supporting and helping them. He was one of those people, no matter how obnoxious he was making himself.

"I'll stop pushing so hard," he promised.

Mallory squinted at him. "I can't help but notice it's not a promise to leave Merrick alone."

"That's because I can't promise that. I want him, and I'm sure he wants me, too. It'll be just some fun between two adults."

"Is it fun if he wants to strangle you the entire time?"

Alpin laughed. "Definitely. You should try angry sex with your dragon."

Mallory shook his head, but he was smiling. Alpin went to work next to him, and together, they quickly filled the trash bag Mallory had been holding. Alpin took it from his brother, closed it, and headed toward the back of the club to leave it outside with the rest of the trash.

That was when he noticed Merrick sneaking toward the back hallway, precisely in the direction he'd been going.

As far as Alpin knew, the office was still mostly intact, as was the rest of the area in the back, and that seemed to be where Merrick was headed. Maybe he needed some time alone to wrap his mind around everything that had happened to his club and his life.

Or maybe he needed a distraction, which Alpin was more than happy to provide.

There was a bounce in his step as he headed outside to throw away the trash.

Seeing all of this, knowing how much work would be needed to get the club back to its former glory, was almost too much. Merrick needed a minute on his own, so he headed toward the office.

That was the one thing that had survived the fire. The clan had set fire to the club's main area, and it had gone up in flames, including the apartment on top of it. Merrick and Arlen had lost almost everything, but the office, which had been a safe place before, was still standing. Everyone knew to stay away from it, which meant Merrick would be left alone, at least for a bit. Even if someone noticed he wasn't cleaning up with the others, they wouldn't look for him.

That was what he needed right now, and he'd been planning on sitting behind the desk, drinking from whatever bottle of spirits Arlen had hidden in the bottom drawer and breathing through the pain.

He just managed to get into the office before he had to lean against the wall. He closed his eyes, taking a deep breath, but the only thing he could smell was smoke. It made his stomach churn, and for one moment, he almost shifted. He needed to get away from the club and the pain all of this created, and the easiest way to make that happen would be to fly. It was the middle of the night, since most of the vampires had wanted to help, so few humans would see him, and those who did would probably think they were dreaming. Merrick would be free for a moment, and he needed that.

But he couldn't leave. Everyone was doing so much for him and Arlen, and it wouldn't be fair to abandon them to do all the work on their own. They deserved for Merrick to be right there with them, which was what he'd do.

As soon as he managed to wrap his mind around the pain and anger.

"Merrick?"

Merrick managed to press his lips together before a groan could escape his throat. What was Alpin doing here? Had he followed Merrick?

Of course he had. Merrick had been watching him—so he

could hide when Alpin looked for him, not because he found Alpin interesting or cute—and he knew how stubborn the vampire could be.

"I know you're here somewhere. I saw you sneaking away. Are you hiding?"

What would Alpin do if Merrick told him that, yes, he was hiding? He'd probably offer to hide with him, which was the last thing Merrick wanted or needed. How could he make Alpin see that? He wasn't sure it was possible, and he had no idea how to get Alpin to understand that he needed to be left alone.

Hiding wouldn't help, and neither would telling Alpin to fuck off. Still, Merrick had to try.

He glared at the door, which he hadn't locked, unfortunately. "Leave me alone," he ordered.

He heard Alpin's footsteps come closer and quickly reached for the door. He was still in time to lock it, and even though it would leave Alpin outside, probably yelling at Merrick to open it, Merrick didn't have to obey. Maybe it would do Alpin good to have someone go against what he wanted. He needed to be put in his place, and while Merrick didn't want to have to do that, for now, it would be enough.

"You know, it's pretty rude of you to hide," Alpin said. "Everyone is here for you. We came to help you set the club to rights, yet, you're hiding. How is that fair?"

Merrick grabbed the door handle, but instead of keeping it shut and locking it, he threw it open. Alpin was on the other side, looking like the cat that ate the cannery.

Dammit. Merrick should have known better. He *had* known better, but for some reason, Alpin got under his skin. He couldn't avoid doing what Alpin wanted.

"You need to leave me alone," he said through gritted teeth.

"Do I? I don't think you should be alone. I think you should be surrounded by people who love you and who want to help you."

"So not you."

Alpin pressed a hand on his chest, right over his heart. "I'm wounded. Why wouldn't I be one of those people? I care about you as much as I care about Arlen."

"Which is not at all, because you don't know us."

"It doesn't mean I don't care." His tone was more serious.

Merrick wasn't sure he should trust it.

"Arlen is part of our family now," Alpin continued. "He's with Mallory, and Mallory's my brother. You come with Arlen since you're *his* family, which means you belong with us. Everyone is worried about you."

Merrick crossed his arms over his chest. "I don't need anyone to be worried about me. I'm perfectly fine, or I will be as soon as you leave me alone."

"But that would be no fun," Alpin replied with a grin.

Merrick had had enough. He and his dragon were fighting over what to do to Alpin, and it made Merrick snap. The dragon wanted to slam Alpin against the wall and fuck him, but Merrick wanted to strangle him. Instead, he snarled at Alpin, showing his fangs. Usually, that was enough to freak people out, especially when they knew he was a dragon shifter. They didn't expect him to also be a vampire, but unfortunately, Alpin already knew about that. He wasn't scared or even offended.

He leaned closer, trying to take a good look at Merrick's fangs. Merrick pressed his lips together, glaring, not understanding why Alpin looked disappointed.

"I want to see them," Alpin whined.

"And I don't want to show them to you."

"Why not? Do you hate them?"

"Don't you?"

Alpin blinked. "Why should I hate my fangs?"

"Because they're a sign that you're a vampire. They're what you use to feed." Thankfully, Merrick could still eat normal food. He wasn't sure what he would have done otherwise.

"So? I don't hate being a vampire."

That wasn't something Merrick could understand. Even though his creator was dead, Merrick still hated him for what he'd done. If he could, he'd dig up the body and kill him again. Instead, he had to deal with his anger in a different way, and he still hadn't found one that worked.

Alpin frowned. "Wait. You hate being a vampire?"

"I don't understand why you don't."

"Because it's impossible to hate. It's given me immortality. I'm not that old yet, but I can imagine everything I'll be able to see by being a vampire, and I can't wait."

"What about your family? You'll lose all of them, and you won't ever grow old. That means you'll have to leave them if you don't want them to see that."

The smile finally vanished from Alpin's face. "I don't care about my family. They can't die soon enough."

Merrick was taken aback, but maybe he shouldn't be. The only person he was close to was Arlen, and they were both dragon shifters, which meant they'd live longer lives than humans.

Well, that would have been the case before. Merrick didn't know how being a vampire would impact the length of his life, and he wasn't looking forward to finding out. He didn't want to lose Arlen. He didn't want to lose anyone who mattered to him, and unfortunately for Arlen, he was the only one who did.

"So you do take some things seriously," Merrick said. He wanted to ask why Alpin hated his family so much, but he suspected Alpin wouldn't take it well. Maybe it would finally push him away, but Merrick couldn't hurt him that way.

Alpin was annoying, but he didn't deserve to be hurt.

"Who said I didn't?"

"You don't seem to. Why can't you leave me alone? I already told you I want nothing to do with you. I came here to get some peace, but you followed me. What can I do to make it stop? Pay you? Kick your ass?"

Alpin stared at Merrick for a moment. His expression told Merrick he wouldn't like whatever came out of his mouth next.

"Kiss me," Alpin eventually said.

"A kiss? That's all you want to leave me alone?" Merrick had a hard time believing that.

"That's not what I meant. Kiss me, and I'll leave you alone if there's no chemistry between us."

"And if there *is* chemistry?"

"Then we'll take it from there."

Merrick didn't want to do it because he knew how good they could be together. Sparks had been flying since the first time they met, even though he'd been ignoring them.

He was tired of resisting. He was tired of telling himself he needed to stay away because Alpin would complicate his life. His life was already complicated as it was.

What could one more mistake do?

Alpin already knew he and Merrick had crazy chemistry. That was the only reason he'd asked Merrick to kiss him. One kiss wouldn't be enough for either of them.

Now, he just had to see if Merrick agreed.

He stared at the dragon shifter, not one bit intimidated, even though Merrick was much bigger than he was. He'd always liked bigger men, and knowing that Merrick was both a dragon shifter and a vampire gave Alpin a thrill. Merrick wouldn't hurt him, but he was dangerous. Maybe it made

Alpin weird, but he had to find his thrill somewhere. He was immortal, after all. It was easy to get bored.

Merrick was still pissed. Alpin could see it from the set of his jaw and the way he was staring. Merrick's intense gaze made Alpin want to shiver, but he knew better than to show Merrick how affected he was. Still, he suspected Merrick knew, but he wasn't about to confirm anything. Better Merrick thought he only wanted sex.

"A kiss?"

Alpin smirked. "Unless you're afraid to kiss me? I mean, I don't think I'm scary, but you're terrified of feelings. It would make sense for you not to want to try this. I wouldn't blame you, but I also wouldn't stop coming after you. I want my answer."

"You know how before you said you hated me?"

Alpin wasn't surprised Merrick remembered his words. "I wasn't serious."

"Well, I am. I hate you."

It shouldn't hurt the way it did. Alpin didn't care about Merrick. He just cared about getting in his pants. Still, the flash of pain deep in his chest made him wonder if there was something more. He wasn't used to feeling anything, but maybe that was what was happening. Maybe that was why he was so focused on getting Merrick in his bed.

He didn't have time to examine his feelings, which he was grateful for. He didn't do well with feelings and didn't understand how anyone could. He liked how Merrick distracted him by grabbing and slamming him against the wall. They were in the office, noses almost touching, staring at each other. Alpin grinned, wondering what was about to happen and excited to find out. Merrick didn't seem happy. He was fierce, though, and that was enough to make Alpin feel satisfied.

Then, Merrick's mouth descended on him.

Alpin squeaked and clung onto Merrick's shoulders as hard as he could. If this was his only chance to get a kiss from Merrick, he wanted to make the most out of it. Hopefully, Merrick would give him more.

The heat between them flared, Alpin's cock heavy and already hard in his jeans. He was pretty sure he could come just from this, and he was eager to find out. He wasn't sure he'd have a chance to until Merrick lowered his hands to cup his ass. Alpin took the opportunity to hop up, needing to be closer, and Merrick got the hint. Alpin wrapped his legs around Merrick's waist, and Merrick pressed him harder against the wall, pushing the breath out of him.

God, Merrick's lips were sinful, and his hands even more so. His touch was enough to drive Alpin nuts and to make him want more. He'd known one taste wouldn't be enough, but just like Merrick, he'd hoped.

That hope had been dashed.

Merrick was kissing him hard, pushing him against the wall to the point of pain. He was hard in his jeans, just like Alpin, and it made Alpin want more. He wished they were somewhere else, somewhere with a bed. He wanted Merrick to come all over him, to use him and mark him as his. This was nothing like what Alpin was used to, and it terrified him.

Usually, sex was nice, and a distraction, but nothing else. This, whatever it was, was already different, and he and Merrick had only kissed. Both of them still had on all their clothes, and Alpin was pretty sure Merrick had no intention of taking one stitch of clothing off. He was focused on getting what he wanted from Alpin, even though Alpin had no idea what that was.

One of Merrick's fangs nicked Alpin's lower lip. He moaned, and when Merrick started moving away, no doubt tasting blood, Alpin buried his hands into Merrick's hair and pulled him closer. He wouldn't give him the time to think about what they were doing and regret it. He wanted Merrick, and now he was sure Merrick wanted him. They were both adults, so there was nothing to stop them from doing what they were doing.

Except maybe sanity.

Their kiss tasted like blood, but that made Alpin's cock harden even more. The head rubbed against his underwear, the sensation both maddening and not enough. Merrick's cock was hard, too, and it pressed against Alpin's, silently begging to come closer. Alpin reached between them, intent to at least open their jeans, but Merrick quickly let go of his ass and grabbed his wrist. He slammed it against the wall, taking control, almost making Alpin come right then and there.

Instead, he kissed Merrick harder, and Merrick kissed him right back. They pressed against each other, needing more and wanting everything the other was willing to offer. Their lips never left each other as they rutted against the wall, yearning for the sweet release they both knew was coming.

Merrick shuddered and pressed Alpin harder against the wall. Alpin knew he had to be content with what Merrick was giving him, so he thrust against Merrick, wiggling his hips so his cock rubbed against his boxer briefs. He needed that friction if he wanted to come. He wasn't sure Merrick would give him enough time, and he didn't want to be left unsatisfied.

Or maybe Merrick would be an honorable man and make sure Alpin came, too. Alpin didn't know and wasn't willing to sacrifice his pleasure to find out.

Merrick stopped kissing Alpin, but he still didn't look at him. Instead, he leaned down, pressing his face against Alpin's neck. Alpin felt the brush of fangs against the sensitive skin there, and that was all he needed. Between that and the thrusts that were harder and faster, almost as if Merrick was trying to make them one, pleasure exploded behind his eyelids.

He hadn't even realized he'd closed his eyes, and he forced himself to open them, even though he couldn't see Merrick well from his position. The only thing he could do was stare at the wall in front of him. His entire world was Merrick, and even though they'd done more than kissing, it still wasn't enough.

Merrick cried out against Alpin's neck, and Alpin felt him bite. He moaned, wondering if he could come again so soon. He was willing to try, but he wasn't surprised that Merrick wasn't.

Only seconds later, he pushed away from Alpin, and Alpin dropped to the floor, almost falling on his face. The only reason he didn't was that he caught himself on the wall. His legs felt like jelly, and he wasn't sure they worked.

He could see the rejection coming, and it hurt. He didn't want Merrick to see how much, so he leaned against the wall, making sure to appear satisfied. "I haven't come in my pants since I was a teenager," he drawled.

Merrick's entire body stiffened. He looked down at himself as if he expected to find his jeans dirty, but there was nothing to be seen. He was safe to go home and find clean clothes, and no one would know what happened.

Alpin was sorry about that. He wasn't one to brag about his conquests, but he didn't want Merrick to go back to ignoring him. For some reason, that hurt.

Merrick was breathing hard and not saying anything. Alpin felt the need to fill the silence. "Well, I don't think either of us can say we don't have chemistry."

Merrick twirled toward him, his expression distorted by anger. "I told you to stay away from me," he snarled.

Alpin wasn't afraid, but he *was* wary. "I didn't force you to do anything," he pointed out.

"Just leave me alone. Stay away from me."

Alpin wanted to tell him he wasn't going to do that, and he didn't care if it made Merrick angrier.

But Merrick was already through the office door, which they'd left open. He didn't look back as he rushed down the hallway, and Alpin didn't call out after him, even though he wanted to.

He leaned against the wall, slowly sliding down until his ass hit the floor. He tilted his head to stare at the ceiling, wondering what the fuck had just happened.

Well, he knew what had happened. He and Merrick had sex, and it was the hottest sex he'd ever had. Still, he wasn't one for repeats. He'd gotten what he wanted, which meant he was supposed to be satisfied now.

And he was. Really, he was.

Chapter Two

"What about insurance?" Merrick asked. He leaned back in his chair, glad that he and Arlen were alone for once. They shared a home in pack territory, but Mallory lived with them, and more often than not, some of his family members were hanging around the house. Today, it was just Merrick and Arlen sitting at the table in the kitchen, sipping coffee.

From the look Arlen gave him, Merrick was pretty sure he'd already told him about this. Merrick hadn't been able to focus on anything lately, and he blamed it on Alpin. He wasn't about to explain that to Arlen, though. His best friend would want to know what had happened, and the last thing Merrick needed was to tell anyone he and Alpin had had sex against a wall.

Arlen wrinkled his nose. "They're still working on it, but the woman I talked to said there were good chances they'd give us the entire amount."

"Really?"

"Yeah. Apparently, the inspectors they sent were clear that it didn't seem criminal, or at least, no accelerants were used. We also have witnesses that we weren't in the club's main area when it started, so we're not suspects."

Merrick snorted. "Did no one mention the dragons?"

"I think many people either want to believe they didn't see them or truly didn't see much. Once the fire started, everyone panicked. They got out as soon as possible and didn't look back. There's a high chance that most people didn't see the clan dragons."

Merrick had been waiting for the other shoe to drop when it came to that. Humans didn't know about supernatural creatures, at least most of them. He had no doubt that some were aware, mostly because they had family members or people they loved involved in their world. Most humans were unaware, and it was best to keep things that way. Having dragons setting the club on fire in front of a bunch of humans wasn't going to help with that.

"And the insurance company had nothing to say about dragons?"

"They didn't mention them, and I wasn't about to ask. I didn't want to risk it."

Merrick leaned back in his chair. "What about the construction company?"

He'd always let Arlen do his thing when it came to business. Arlen was much better at it than Merrick could ever hope to be, and that was fine with him. When the club had been open, Merrick had taken care of hiring people, both for the bar and security. He wanted to go back to that, but unfortunately, until they could rebuild, he was out of his depth. It wasn't new since he'd gone through this already before they'd opened.

What was happening right now felt so similar to what happened in the past that it was odd. The only difference was that Arlen had a boyfriend, and they were surrounded by people who considered them family. Merrick had a hard time wrapping his mind around that and accepting it, but he couldn't deny it, especially when he looked at Arlen and Mallory. He was glad they'd found each other. Arlen deserved to be happy more than many people Merrick knew. If a vampire made that happen, then Merrick liked that vampire.

But not all of them.

"All right, why don't you tell me why you're so

distracted," Arlen suddenly said.

Merrick was pretty sure he'd missed something else. "Aren't you? With everything that happened, I'm having a hard time focusing. I'm still pissed at the clan and want them to pay for what they did, but I don't know how to make that happen."

"Maybe you *shouldn't* make it happen. It's not really your place."

"I'm sorry, but aren't we involved with a group of people who are planning to do just that?"

"Yes, and we'll help them, but it's not your personal crusade. Don't go out there and try to deal with the clan on your own, please." Arlen leaned forward, pushing the papers they'd been going over away. "You matter too much to me. I don't want anything to happen to you because you wanted revenge."

Merrick looked away. He cared about Arlen, and Arlen cared about him. He was still uncomfortable with emotions and wasn't quite sure how to deal with them. Arlen never had that problem, and now that he was with Mallory, he seemed to be saying *I love you* to anyone who listened.

"I won't do anything stupid," he promised.

At least not when it came to the clan. Merrick wasn't an idiot, and he knew that he had no chance to do anything on his own. He wasn't gunning for the clan, mostly because he didn't have a death wish.

But he *was* an idiot when it came to Alpin. He'd already known that one time with the vampire wouldn't be enough, and he was right. Even though they'd had sex at the club, Merrick's hands itched to get back on Alpin, possibly on his naked skin this time. It wasn't going to happen, but he couldn't help but wonder if Alpin felt the same. He'd seemed convinced they'd have chemistry, and he was right, but he didn't strike Merrick as a relationship kind of guy. That probably meant he wouldn't want a repeat, which Merrick should be happy about—and he was.

Or at least, he was trying to convince himself of that.

"There you go again," Arlen said, tapping his fingertips on the table. "I thought you were thinking about the clan, but I'm not so sure anymore. What's going on in that head of yours when you disappear in your thoughts? Is it really about the club and what happened?"

Merrick didn't want to involve Arlen in this. Knowing his best friend, Arlen would be happy that Merrick had finally found someone, even though that wasn't so. He wouldn't understand that what happened with Alpin was a one-time thing, and he'd imagine Merrick and Alpin living together and being happy, adopting a string of baby dragons and new vampires.

The thought almost made Merrick roll his eyes. Relationships weren't for him. Arlen, sure, but not him. No one was going to change that, not even an adorable vampire who'd gotten under his skin.

Thankfully, Merrick's phone vibrated on the table, and he snatched it up, eager to get out of the conversation. His eyes widened at the sight of the text message on his screen, and when he looked up, his gaze crossed Arlen's.

They both shot out of their chair at the same time. The pack needed them.

They were under attack.

They rushed out, not hesitating to go to the help of the wolf shifters. The wolves had welcomed them when they hadn't had anyone or anything in the world, and it meant something to both Arlen and Merrick. No matter what was happening, Merrick would die trying to help the pack.

Although he hoped it wouldn't come to that.

"You have any more details than I do?" he asked as they ran.

Arlen shook his head. "The text just said where the attack was happening."

And they were headed that way. The problem was that they didn't know who was attacking, which meant they had no idea what they'd be faced with. It could be other wolf shifters, vampires, or dragons. The fact that it probably was the last one was terrifying, but Merrick was ready to fight.

It took them about five minutes to reach the spot where the attack had happened, and Merrick was relieved to see it was already over. That meant no dragons were involved, and the wolf shifters on patrol had been able to subdue whoever had been attacking. A few of them were wounded, but someone was already taking care of them. A dead wolf in their wolf form was on the ground, and Merrick hoped that whoever it was wasn't a pack member.

"What happened?" he asked as he strode toward the body.

A wolf shifter he recognized stepped forward to explain. "They attacked," he explained. "There were four of them, and the other three escaped."

"Is it anyone you know?"

Ollis's expression told Merrick that was the case. "The attackers were some of the people who left the clan with Fay and the old alpha."

Merrick grimaced. "I'm sorry."

Ollis shook his head. "They shouldn't have left us. They *definitely* shouldn't have attacked us."

He wasn't wrong, but it still couldn't be easy to have to kill someone they'd considered family until recently.

The place was a mess. More wolves kept coming, and Kieran was there, too, doing his job as the alpha. His brother was present, as well, ordering people around and sending them home when they weren't needed. Merrick felt like an idiot, standing there with nothing to do, so he moved toward the little group that had gathered around Kieran. Most of the vampires were there, including Alpin, and Merrick did his best not to look his way.

"We can help," Tyrian was saying. "We live here currently, and it's not right for your wolves to have to protect us, too. All of you are exhausted, and the least we can do is help you patrol pack territory."

"Us, too," Merrick declared, knowing Arlen would be okay with it. "Let us help."

Kieran sighed. "We can have a meeting to talk about this once this mess is cleaned up. Why don't you head to my house? Robin will want to know what happened, and he'll get something to eat together for everyone."

The night was far from over, but Merrick, Arlen, and the vampires were used to staying up until dawn. They'd have time to come up with a plan that would keep the pack safe.

They had to.

Alpin didn't like any of this. The pack was his brother's home, and Mallory needed to be safe. Having wolves attack in the middle of the night, when most of the shifters were sleeping, wasn't a great way to make that happen.

But like always, Tyrian had stepped in, and Alpin trusted him. He'd made the right decision for Mallory and for the pack, and Alpin would follow his orders. There was a reason Tyrian was their creator and Alpin considered him his father.

"I don't like involving you in this," Kieran said.

They'd all gathered in his living room, in the house where he lived with Robin, a vampire. Robin wasn't part of their family, but Alpin liked him and didn't want anything to happen to him or Kieran. Hell, most of the wolves were growing on him. They deserved to be safe in their territory, but it was getting harder, partly because of the dragon clan.

"We're already involved," Arlen said. "What's happening

with the dragons is partly our fault, and Merrick and I feel guilty about your pack being in the crossfire. I'd offer for us to leave, but something tells me it wouldn't be enough to get the dragons to look away. That means the pack would be in danger anyway, so we might as well stay and help defend it."

"And since Mallory and Arlen are part of our family, we'll do the same," Tyrian declared. He looked around at the people he considered family, including Alpin, and they all nodded.

Alpin was on board with helping the wolves. If anything, it gave him something to focus on, and he wouldn't be bored.

But he wasn't in this just for that reason. He wanted his brother to be happy and live a peaceful life, and that wouldn't happen with a dragon clan breathing down his neck and threatening everything he and his boyfriend were building. The clan had already taken away Arlen's livelihood. That wouldn't be enough to keep Arlen down, but Alpin had no doubt that the clan wasn't done with him and Merrick.

He swallowed. That was one man he didn't want to think about. He'd been forcing himself not to since that day at the club, but it was becoming harder. He'd never wanted a repeat as badly as he did now, and he wasn't sure how to deal with it. If it had been anyone else, he'd have just fucked them again without explaining himself. The problem was that Merrick wasn't just a guy. He was technically part of Alpin's family, which meant that if things went badly, everyone would suffer.

"All right," Kieran said. Even though he'd protested, he looked relieved now that he was accepting their help. "What are you willing to do?"

"You're the alpha. You tell us what you want to use us for and where you need us. In this situation, consider us your pack members."

It was odd to hear Tyrian talk that way. He'd always been

the leader of their coven, which meant he was usually the one giving orders. In this case, Alpin thought he was right to give that honor and complication to Kieran. It was Kieran's territory and his wolves who were being attacked, after all.

Kieran slowly nodded. "I think it would be best to divide everyone into teams of two. I won't touch the normal patrols, but I'll add the people present tonight to the same areas. You won't be working with the wolves but rather alongside them. That way, if anyone is attacked, the others will be able to step in quickly. Each pair will have their own area."

Alpin nodded as Kieran started splitting people into pairs. He expected to be paired up with one of his siblings, which was fine with him. He worked well with most of them, and they were used to dealing with him.

His brain froze when he heard the name paired with his.

"Alpin, I'd like you to work with Merrick," Kieran said.

Alpin forced himself not to look at the dragon shifter. "I'm sorry?"

"Merrick," Kieran repeated, staring at Alpin. "I don't want to pair our two dragon shifters because I believe they'll be more useful divided. It also makes them less of a target."

Alpin agreed, but did Kieran really have to pair him with Merrick? "I can work with someone else. I don't have to be with one of the dragons."

"I agree. I can work with any of the vampires," Merrick quickly said.

He was avoiding looking at Alpin, which wasn't a surprise.

Kieran arched a brow. "Is there a good reason for you to be paired with someone else?"

"Well, no, but surely, there's no good reason to pair us together," Alpin said.

"Actually, there is. I considered everyone's strengths and weaknesses, which is why I think the two of you together makes sense. Unless there's a reason you shouldn't be? I mean, I didn't pair Mallory with Arlen. I don't want to put them in that kind of situation. If the two of you are together, I can pair you with someone else."

"We're not," Merrick quickly said.

Kieran nodded. "Then there's no reason for you not to work together."

Alpin wasn't surprised when Merrick got to his feet. "Fine. I'll work with him as long as he can be serious and actually do the job," he snapped.

"I'm sure it won't be a problem," Kieran said, clearly trying to soothe Merrick. "But if you really don't want to work with Alpin, I can put you with someone else."

"It's *fine*. You're the alpha, and whatever you decide is the law."

"Maybe, but it's not how we do things here."

"I'll work with Alpin. Now, if you'll excuse me, I have to make a phone call."

Alpin watched Merrick leave the room. He was pretty sure there was no phone call, but he wasn't about to call Merrick out on that. He kind of wanted to run, too, but it would make it even more obvious to everyone in the room that something was happening. They were already staring and no doubt wanting to ask what was going on.

Alpin hadn't told anyone what had happened at the club with Merrick. He wasn't planning on doing so, and he'd been trying to convince himself that now that he and Merrick had sex, he could stop thinking about the dragon. He *wanted* to stop thinking about him.

Yet, it felt impossible to do so.

"What happened with Merrick?" Mallory asked, leaning closer to Alpin.

Alpin shook his head. He was tempted to follow Merrick outside, if anything so he could get away from his gossiping siblings, but once again, he knew better. "Nothing. You know he hates me, so that's probably why he doesn't want to work with me."

Mallory stared at Alpin with narrow eyes. "Are you sure that's all there is to it?"

"Of course. What else could there be?"

"I know you. You've been trying to get into Merrick's pants since we arrived. He protested a lot, but it doesn't mean he wasn't agreeable to it."

Alpin snorted. "Can you imagine him saying yes?"

"As a matter of fact, I can. I understand if you don't want to tell me about it, but remember that I'm here if you need to talk. Besides, Arlen knows Merrick better than anyone. If you need help with Merrick, he's the person to talk to."

Alpin cleared his throat. "I'll be fine."

He didn't understand what he was feeling or the way he was behaving. Usually, he didn't have a problem telling his siblings about his conquests. He boasted about how many people he slept with and what they did in bed, but it felt disrespectful to do the same about Merrick, maybe because Merrick was a family friend. Arlen considered him a brother, which meant Merrick was Mallory's brother-in-law.

And in a way, Alpin's brother-in-law. Gosh, what a mess.

Merrick's plan to stay away from Alpin had failed spectacularly. How was he supposed to do that when he'd been forced to work with him? There was no explaining to Kieran why it was a better idea to keep them as far away from each other as possible, so the only thing Merrick could do was pace the forest and try to get the anger to fade enough that he wouldn't kill Alpin the next time he saw him.

He hated all of this. He hated that Alpin had such a big influence on him, that he could make him feel this way. He didn't like being out of control, which was precisely how he felt when Alpin was concerned. He wanted Alpin out of his life, but how could he make that happen?

He couldn't. Unless he left Arlen and the club behind, Alpin would always be there. He was Mallory's brother, and there was no changing that, which meant Merrick had to get used to having him around. Maybe they could talk and come to an agreement.

Merrick stopped pacing and tilted his head up to look at the sky. Alpin was chaos personified, but surely, he could agree to keep his distance from Merrick unless it was necessary for them to be together. He had to understand that it was for the best, for both of them and for their family.

Merrick snorted. Would Alpin understand, or would he make both their lives harder? Merrick would have faith if it had been anyone else, but not with Alpin. Unless he felt that he'd gotten what he'd wanted, he'd continue pushing, and Merrick could either give in again or tell him to fuck off and explain everything to Kieran.

Just the thought made him shudder in horror.

So telling Kieran about them was out of the question. They also couldn't avoid working together, which meant they'd have to talk.

"Okay, what's going on?" Arlen asked from behind Merrick, startling him.

He turned to glare at his best friend. "Nothing."

Arlen arched a brow. "Are you really lying to me? You're going to have to try harder, because you're shit at it. I can read you better than I can read myself, and I *know* something's going on."

Merrick wanted to scream. Instead, he stared at Arlen. Why was he resisting telling his best friend about Alpin so hard? He didn't think Arlen would be happy about them having been together, but he'd understand. He knew Merrick better than anyone else in the world, and he was the only one who could give Merrick advice.

"Arlen?" Mallory called out, stepping outside.

Both Arlen and Merrick turned to look at him. He grimaced, then gestured at the inside of the house. "Kieran is talking to everyone."

"We'll be right there," Arlen promised before turning back to Merrick. "You and I will talk about this," he promised. "I don't know what's going on with you, but you can't continue doing whatever this is."

"I'm fine. I promise I'm not going after the clan and will do whatever Kieran asks of me."

"I have no doubt about that." He hesitated. "You don't have to talk to me, but I'm worried, Merrick. You've always been closed off, but it's become worse after everything that happened with the club and the clan. I know I'm not as involved as I was before since meeting Mallory, but I'm here for you."

Merrick hated that he'd made Arlen feel guilty about something he shouldn't feel guilty about. He reached out and squeezed his best friend's shoulder, silently telling him everything was okay. Maybe he shouldn't be too silent about it, though. "I promise I'm fine," he said. "A lot has been happening, and it's confusing and infuriating, and you know I'm not the best at dealing with feelings. I swear I'll talk to you if I need to talk to anyone."

Arlen stared for a moment before nodding. "All right. I'll be waiting until you feel comfortable enough to tell me."

They rejoined the others in Kieran and Robin's living room. Merrick carefully avoided looking toward Alpin. He wasn't sure how he'd react if he made eye contact with the vampire, but he wasn't willing to risk it. Eventually the two of them would have to talk before things exploded in their faces. For now, they had better things to focus on than what was going on in their minds or their pants.

Kieran looked around the room, clearly exhausted. It made Merrick feel guilty about making his job harder, but he'd do pretty much anything not to have to deal with Alpin on a regular basis. Still, they were stuck together for however long this took to resolve, which meant they'd have to learn to spend time together without either killing each other or fucking against a tree.

"Thank you," Kieran said. "I can't tell you how much this means to my pack and me. You have no obligations to us, yet you're here. For a long time, when my father was the alpha, the pack was isolated. I'm glad to see that's not the case anymore, because we need help, and we're ready to help whoever needs it." He paused. "As soon as the dragons aren't trying to kill us, anyway."

That caused a few people in the room to chuckle.

"Now," Kieran continued, "I know most of you didn't anticipate we'd be attacked or expect to be assigned to patrolling pack territory, so it's fine if you're not available tonight, but I'd feel better if at least a few of you could walk around and keep an eye open. I'd also appreciate it if there was anyone you know we could contact who would provide help. The way I see it, what the clan is doing puts every single supernatural creature in danger. We need to protect ourselves and each other and help where we can. We're getting good results reaching out to other packs and supernatural groups, but the more people we manage to contact, the better."

Merrick had every intention of staying silent, but he should have known the same couldn't be said for Arlen. He didn't even look at Merrick as he spoke. "Merrick's coven should probably be warned."

Merrick glared at him. Arlen knew what he was doing, which was no doubt why he was avoiding looking at him. He knew Merrick was pissed and that he'd explode if they so much as glanced at each other.

Kieran frowned and turned his attention to Merrick. "Your coven? I thought you lived with the dragon clan."

Merrick refused to answer, but Arlen had no problem doing so for him. "We did. Merrick spent very little time with the coven, even after the man who turned him into a vampire was killed. That man was evil, but Harmon, the vampire who took his place, is a nice guy. He regularly reaches out to check in on Merrick."

Merrick frowned, because that was news to him. Arlen clearly had kept secrets, and Merrick would make sure his best friend knew what he thought of that.

"The coven is local?"

"More or less. They'll want to know what's happening with the dragons, though. I'm sure Harmon would also want to know that Merrick is in danger."

Merrick and Arlen would *definitely* have words once this meeting was over.

Kieran looked at Merrick. "I can tell by your expression that you don't like that Arlen brought your coven up. That's all right, and I won't force you to work with them, but don't you think that, at the very least, they should be warned about what's happening? The dragons are focused on our pack, but that won't last long. If they want to take over the supernatural world, they'll have to deal with anyone with a bit of power, which probably includes your coven."

Merrick couldn't say he was wrong. He might not know what to make of Harmon and the coven, but that didn't mean he wished for them to be hurt or, worse, killed by the clan. He wasn't sure he could work with Harmon, but maybe he didn't have to, even if Harmon wanted to be involved in what was happening.

Merrick had a coven. Alpin hadn't expected that, but maybe

he should have. Even though he was also a dragon shifter, Merrick *was* a vampire. It sounded like his change into a vampire hadn't been great, which probably was why Merrick looked pissed that Arlen had mentioned the other vampires. Maybe he didn't have much contact with them, which would make sense if his turning had been traumatic.

That happened way too often, and Alpin knew how lucky he'd been that Tyrian had been the one to turn him. He'd been sick, but Tyrian had made sure he knew what he was dealing with and what would happen to him if he became a vampire.

Alpin wanted to know what had happened to Merrick, but he was convinced that if he asked, Merrick would tell him to fuck off. It was obvious that Merrick had been avoiding him, especially tonight, which meant that if Alpin wanted an answer, he'd have to force himself into Merrick's life.

He'd been telling himself he could stay away from Merrick now that he had what he wanted, but he was starting to realize that, for the first time, he needed more. The sex had been great, and he'd be up for a repeat even if there was nothing else, but there had to be a reason that he wanted Merrick so badly. Alpin was a lot most of the time, but he didn't tease anyone the way he teased Merrick, especially not after he had them in his bed. He was curious to find out what more there could be, which would only happen if he and Merrick spent time together.

"Fine," Merrick said, still staring at Kieran. "I'll visit Harmon."

"You could call him."

"I could, but I think this is better delivered face-to-face. Besides, he'll want to see me. It's been a while."

"I'll go with him," Alpin quickly volunteered. If glares could kill, he'd be a pile of ashes just about now, but since Merrick's expression couldn't do anything to him, he beamed and kept his focus on Kieran.

Kieran cocked his head as if he were trying to read Alpin. "It's nice of you to volunteer," he said slowly.

"I know. Besides, if Merrick and I are going to work together to keep the pack safe, we should probably get to know each other better. What better way to do that than meeting his family? He already knows mine, after all."

Kieran looked from Merrick to Alpin. It was clear he could tell something was up, but Alpin doubted he'd ask. He was probably too afraid that Merrick would eat him if he did.

"Well, it would be a relief to know Merrick isn't alone," Kieran eventually said.

"I don't have to be protected when I visit my brother," Merrick snapped.

So he considered this Harmon guy his brother. That was interesting, and it made Alpin want to go with him even more.

"Not while you're there, but where's the coven? Is there a chance the clan could find out you're traveling there and try to stop you, or worse, get rid of you? I don't want to risk it. Alpin volunteered to go with you, and I think it's a good idea. Unless you have a reason it's not?"

Once again, Kieran was telling them to be honest. Alpin was pretty sure from Merrick's expression that he wasn't about to tell him what was going on, which was fine with him at the moment. He wanted to meet Merrick's brother. He had about a dozen questions for him already, and he probably needed to write them down before he forgot.

"Also, if the two of you are free tonight, would you like to patrol pack territory?" Kieran asked when Merrick didn't answer.

"No problem," Alpin said happily.

"I hope you know what you're doing," Mallory whispered from his spot on the couch next to Alpin.

"When don't I know what I'm doing?"

Mallory snorted. "Pretty much always. You throw yourself into situations without thinking about the consequences. I can tell something is happening between you and Merrick, and I respect the fact that you don't want to talk about it, but maybe it would be a good idea not to poke at him too much. You know how he is."

But Alpin didn't, not really. Merrick had been keeping him at arm's length since they'd met, and he understood why, but that only made him more curious. He wanted to find out why Merrick was under his skin, but also what made him angry, happy, and a whole list of other things. If he could get that by visiting Merrick's coven with him, he wouldn't hesitate.

"We can go now," Merrick confirmed.

Alpin jumped to his feet, grinning around. "How exciting."

"It's not exciting," Merrick snapped. "This is a serious job, and if you can't do it, you'd better tell us now. Kieran still has time to replace you."

Alpin scowled at him. "I'll have you know that I'm perfectly able to defend myself and the pack. You can ask Tyrian if you don't believe me. He's the one who trained me."

Merrick shook his head and headed toward the door. He didn't say goodbye to anyone, but Alpin waved around, grinning like an idiot. He felt like one, too. His crush couldn't end well, and it would end in pain if he was unlucky. He wouldn't be surprised if he managed to push Merrick to the point that he tried to strangle him.

He was willing to risk it.

He rushed after Merrick, bouncing behind him as he waited for Merrick to say something. After a while, he realized Merrick wasn't going to give him the time of day. He'd clearly decided to stay silent as they patrolled the edge of pack territory together. It was probably a smart idea, but no one had ever said that Alpin was smart.

"You don't have to walk so quickly," he complained. "My

legs are shorter than yours, and I'm having a hard time keeping up."

Merrick grunted, so he'd heard Alpin, but instead of slowing down, he started moving even faster. Alpin scowled at his back, wondering what he saw in the infuriating man. It was better this way, though. There was nothing lovable about Merrick, and the sooner Alpin could convince himself of that, the better it would be.

He wasn't one for feelings, and there was a reason for that. They hurt. That was why he was so confused by how he felt about Merrick, but it wouldn't last long. He was sure that this ridiculous crush would vanish like it had never existed as soon as he spent a bit of time with Merrick. Then, Alpin could go back to fucking any cute guy he met and forget about Merrick.

And so what if Merrick was the hottest guy Alpin had ever met? And so what if the sex they'd had together made every single other time Alpin had been with someone vanish from his mind? There could be nothing between him and Merrick, and he didn't *want* there to be anything. He was free as a bird, and that was never going to change, not even for a handsome dragon with a hidden side and many secrets.

CHAPTER THREE

This was Merrick's worst nightmare. Not only was he headed to visit the coven, but he was doing so with Alpin in his passenger seat.

What had he done to deserve this?

"You like old people's music," Alpin complained.

He reached over to change the song, and Merrick quickly turned to glare at him. Alpin glared right back, but he raised his hands in surrender and slumped back in his seat.

"Fine. We'll listen to your music. I thought the rule was that the passenger chooses the music."

"The driver and owner of the car does," Merrick drawled.

He was surprised Alpin was giving up so easily. There was no doubt something behind it, and he wasn't looking forward to finding out what that something was. He didn't want to know. If he could help it, he didn't want anything to do with Alpin.

That wasn't going to be easy, considering they were stuck in a car together and would be stuck back in it a few hours later when they headed back toward the city.

Merrick focused on the road in front of him. The coven lived in an isolated compound on the mountain. Before, it had been more like a cult, and while Harmon had done his best to change that, he couldn't change the place where the coven lived. The house was one of the reasons Merrick had left, and he wasn't looking forward to being back. At least his creator was dead and wouldn't be there to make him want to strangle someone.

He already had enough of that with Alpin.

"So, why don't you tell me about your coven?" Alpin said.

He sounded delighted, as if he'd discovered a massive secret Merrick had been hiding. Merrick supposed he had. He'd never told anyone but Arlen about the coven and how he'd been turned into a vampire. It had happened a long time ago. Arlen was the only person he could trust to keep all of his secrets, including the fact that he was part vampire.

Or at least, he'd thought so until Arlen had blurted everything out to Kieran.

No one knew how it worked. Merrick was pretty sure his creator hadn't been convinced it would, but he'd wanted to try, and Merrick had been there. He wasn't the only supernatural being Sigmund had tortured that way. Sometimes, Merrick got so angry at the memories that he wished he could dig up his creator and kill the asshole. Thankfully, Harmon had done the job for him, and Merrick didn't have to worry about the elder vampire butting into his life.

Technically, Merrick was still part of the coven. He always would be, since he'd been turned by its creator. He'd never wanted anything to do with them, and once Harmon had won his challenge and killed Sigmund, Merrick had hightailed it out of there. He'd told himself he would never go back, and he wouldn't have if this hadn't been so important. Unfortunately, it was, which meant he'd have to find a way to deal with it.

"Are you going to tell me anything about them?" Alpin asked.

"No."

Alpin huffed. "I'm sure there are things I should know. For example, Arlen mentioned something about your creator being an asshole. It doesn't sound like he's in charge of the coven anymore, so I'm wondering who challenged and killed him?"

"None of your business," Merrick said through gritted teeth. When would this night end? It couldn't be fast enough.

"All right. Since you won't answer my questions, I'm just going to say things out loud, and you can grunt if I'm right."

Merrick was going to strangle Alpin. He'd have to explain it to Mallory, but he suspected the vampire would understand. He was Alpin's brother, which meant he'd been forced to live with him much longer than Merrick. Honestly, it was a miracle none of the siblings had killed Alpin yet.

"Considering the way you're behaving, I'm going to guess that you didn't leave your coven on the best of terms."

Alpin didn't care what Merrick wanted or thought of him, and Merrick was kind of impressed. Most people would have been terrified of him after he'd shown them his fangs and growled a few times, but not Alpin. He kept talking as if he couldn't see Merrick glowering in the driver's seat.

"But you called the man in charge of the coven your brother, which means you like him," Alpin continued.

"How do you figure that?" Merrick was curious to see where Alpin was going.

"Well, I like all my siblings. Doesn't the same goes for you?"

Merrick snorted, but he didn't answer. Alpin waited for a moment before he realized Merrick wouldn't add anything, then he continued speculating.

"So, since the old leader was an asshole and the new one is your brother, I'm going to guess you were both created by the asshole."

Merrick wasn't going to laugh at what Alpin had just said. He couldn't afford for Alpin to think he liked him.

Even though he did.

He sighed. He should probably give Alpin at least a few details, if anything so he'd be ready when they arrived and know what to expect. He'd ask questions to anyone he met, anyway. At least like this, Merrick could control the information he got. Hopefully, what he had to say would be enough for Alpin.

Merrick realized he was a fool to hope for that.

He cleared his throat, getting Alpin's attention. "Yes, both Harmon and I were created by the same vampire. Harmon was already there when I arrived. I've been part of the clan since I was born in it, but Sigmund didn't care. He saw something he wanted, and he decided to take it. I was much younger then, and I didn't think to be careful. I almost died because of it. Sigmund dragged me here and turned me. I had no idea what was happening, and Harmon was the one who took care of me."

It was hard to think back to those memories, which was one of the reasons Merrick avoided coming here like the plague—even though the plague wouldn't actually hurt him.

"I think that seeing what Sigmund did to me was the thing that pushed Harmon to the edge," he continued. "He'd already been unhappy with the way Sigmund guided the coven, and he knew the man was losing his mind. You'll see when we get to the coven, but it was more like a cult than anything else. I honestly don't understand why Harmon still lives up this mountain. He could move the coven, but I guess this place holds memories for him." Possibly better memories than Merrick's.

Or maybe Harmon didn't have anyone else. He was the coven's leader, which meant he was in charge of protecting them. He couldn't just drop everyone and leave. Most of the coven members didn't deserve for him to do that. They'd never been on their creator's side. They'd been along for the ride because they hadn't had a choice.

"Anyway, I was an experiment for Sigmund," Merrick added. "After a while, I'd had enough. I wanted to go home, and the only way for me to do that was to kill the asshole, or at least, that was what it felt like. I had no idea that it would have meant I'd become the leader, and it would have freaked me out if I had. Luckily, Harmon knew what I was planning, and he stepped in. He challenged Sigmund, won, and the rest is history. He's been in charge of the coven since then, and as far as I know, he's doing a great job."

"So he's not the reason you refuse to go back," Alpin commented.

Merrick took one last turn, and the compound appeared in front of them. Alpin sucked in a breath, suddenly silent, which made Merrick smile.

If he'd known taking Alpin up the mountain would be enough to keep him quiet, he'd have done it days ago.

Alpin was in awe, and not just of the house hanging on the side of the mountain in front of him. He couldn't believe Merrick had told him everything he'd just said. He didn't think he'd ever heard the man talk so much, and he was tempted to ask more questions just so he could continue listening to Merrick's voice.

He knew better than to do that.

Merrick would realize what he was doing and clam up again. Right now, they were at an okay point in their relationship—if they could even call what they had a relationship. Merrick had opened up about his past, and Alpin had listened. Hopefully, Merrick had finally realized he could trust Alpin, although Alpin wasn't holding his breath.

Still, trust or no trust, Alpin knew more about Merrick than most people, or at least, he suspected so. He realized it was only because he was the one here rather than someone else, but he didn't care. Merrick had told him a lot of stuff, and he was proud to have been trusted.

"Are there things I need to know?" he asked.

"What do you mean? Didn't I tell you enough?"

Alpin rolled his eyes. He hadn't expected Merrick to have miraculously changed, and he was right. "I meant about the clan, its power dynamics, and the people who live here. What kind of leader is Harmon?"

"He's good. He's not cruel and doesn't force anyone to stay or leave. I know he had some problems early on with some of Sigmund's followers, but he nipped those problems in the bud, and the coven has been peaceful since then. The people who wanted to leave did, although I'm sure most are still coven members like I am. There haven't been new additions because, as far as I know, Harmon doesn't turn people. You don't need to worry about anyone. They won't try to hurt or attack you."

Alpin snorted. "I'd like to see them try. Tyrian would make sure they regret it."

"He cares a lot about you," Merrick said in what sounded like a wistful tone.

"He does. He cares about all of us."

Alpin was surprised he and Merrick were having what seemed to be a normal conversation, and he wasn't quite sure how to deal with it. He was used to using humor and pushing people into not taking him seriously. That was what he'd done with Merrick, too, but he wondered if maybe Merrick could see right through him. He wouldn't be the first, but the only other people who knew Alpin well enough to be aware that his bubbly personality was mostly a mask he used when he wasn't sure what to do were part of his family. They'd never hurt Alpin, but he wasn't quite sure about Merrick.

He doubted Merrick would hurt him intentionally. If Alpin pushed him too hard, he might snap at him in anger, but it would be Alpin's fault.

The problem was that Alpin didn't know what he wanted. There was something different about Merrick, and Alpin wished to find out what that thing was, but he was also terrified. He couldn't recognize himself, and it had something to do with the way he felt around Merrick. He had no idea what they were doing or how to deal with it, and while his first instinct was to continue poking at Merrick until the man snapped, he pressed his lips together and told himself not to be an idiot.

Did the reason why he wanted Merrick to think well of him matter? As long as he was in time to correct his behavior, he could show Merrick he wasn't an idiot with a head full of air. He might not be as good a fighter as Mallory, but then he'd never been an enforcer. That didn't mean he didn't train, and he knew how to hold his own in a fight.

Not that they were expecting a fight. Even though Merrick was clearly uncomfortable with what his creator had done, he sounded fine when he talked about Harmon. The few details he'd given Alpin made Alpin believe that Harmon was fond of Merrick, too, so there was a good chance they'd be more than welcome with the coven.

The house on the mountain became bigger as they drove closer. Alpin had never met a silence he couldn't break, so he continued asking questions about the house. He could tell Merrick was done giving him personal details, but surely, he could talk about this place.

"I don't know who built it," Merrick explained, a hint of impatience in his tone. "It was already there when I arrived, and I suspect it'll stay standing for a long time."

"But I want to know why this person built this thing. Is it ancient?"

"It depends on what you mean by ancient. Look, I don't have any details. You should probably ask Harmon if you want to know more, but for now, could you maybe shut up?"

"You're *asking* me to be silent?" Alpin almost gasped. "I can't believe you're asking instead of ordering."

"Don't make me change my mind," Merrick grumbled.

Alpin realized he was pushing, but he couldn't help it. He *liked* pushing Merrick. It was the only time Merrick seemed alive, and as far as Alpin was concerned, he was doing it for everyone, not only himself. Harmon cared a lot about Merrick, so he'd be happy if Merrick communicated better, right? Alpin would never be able to change Merrick's personality, but he could try to soften it.

He wasn't sure it was his place or if he had what it took to do something like that, but he was willing to try. He was about to be introduced to Merrick's brother.

He was tempted to continue talking, but instead, he stared at the house on the mountain. It was more like a castle, really. It was clear that whoever had it built had been inspired by something they'd probably seen in Europe.

It looked medieval, all in gray stone, half between a grand house and a castle, with a round tower that appeared more recently built and overlooked everything. It was right on the edge of the mountain, looking as if a strong breeze might push it over. The only way to get inside seemed to be a wood and stone bridge, and Alpin realized he was right when Merrick eventually parked in a wide opening that was full of other vehicles. The bridge was small, so clearly, it was only for foot traffic.

It was impressive. Alpin hadn't lived that long, even though he was a vampire, but he'd never seen anything like this. He couldn't help but wonder what the person who'd built it had been inspired by and where that place was. He was tempted to ask just so he could visit, but it wasn't like he'd be able to go anytime soon. Mallory needed him and the rest of his family.

But it went straight on Alpin's bucket list.

It wasn't a list of things to do before he died, since he couldn't die anymore, just a list of things he'd never have been able to do when he was human. With Tyrian and the rest of his family at his back, Alpin could do whatever he wanted now, and he took advantage of that. He could live life in a way he could never have dreamed of.

"It's a bit dramatic," Merrick said as he rubbed the back of his neck.

Alpin peered at the castle. "I'm not sure what I should call it, but *house* isn't the right word."

"But it's a home for the coven, which is like a big family."

Merrick was flustered, and it was both amusing and endearing. "I know what a coven is. Mine is my family. I realize we're much smaller than most covens, but that's how it should be."

"Anyway. Are you ready to go in?"

"Lead the way. I'll follow you anywhere."

Merrick grumbled, but he got out of the car, and Alpin hurried to follow his lead. Merrick locked the car, then strode toward the short bridge that would lead them inside. Alpin bounced as he followed. This was an adventure he hadn't expected, and he always loved those.

They hadn't even reached the other side of the bridge when the massive door there opened. It was wooden, making Alpin want to grab an ax, scream, and throw himself at it as if he were trying to conquer the castle. Maybe he could even have a helmet or something.

It was a good thing he couldn't do it, because a tall man stepped out.

There was no resemblance with Merrick. They weren't actually related, even though the same vampire had turned them. But the way the handsome man smiled was enough to tell Alpin he was Harmon, Merrick's brother.

He was handsome. His long brown hair was tied on the back of his neck, and his brown eyes glittered in the light from the lamp just above the door. He was almost as tall as Merrick, but where Merrick's shoulders were broad and he was muscled, Harmon was slender. Alpin had no doubt that Harmon could kick his ass without a second thought, though, so he promised himself he'd behave. If he wanted Merrick to like him, he'd have to get Harmon to do so, too.

And he would.

Merrick hated that he was back here, so he was surprised at how happy he was to see Harmon again. They hadn't spent much time together, just under a year before Harmon had killed Sigmund. Still, during that time, Harmon had been the only one who wasn't too scared of Sigmund to take care of Merrick. He'd taught him everything he could about being a vampire and what it meant, but even he had no idea how being both a dragon and vampire would impact Merrick's life. Still, he'd been the only one who tried, and Merrick would always be grateful for that.

Harmon beamed, and as soon as Merrick was close enough, opened his arms. Merrick didn't even think about saying no. He wrapped his arms around Harmon, pulling his brother close. His shifter side meant that the first thing he did was sniff Harmon, which made Harmon chuckle. Merrick could feel his body shake, and it made him smile.

When he stepped back, Alpin gasped, getting Harmon's attention.

"You're smiling," Alpin said, staring at Merrick.

Merrick glared at him. Alpin raised a finger and poked at Merrick's cheek.

"And it's gone," Alpin said. He pouted. "It's a pity because you're pretty when you smile."

"I already told you not to tell me to smile," Merrick snapped.

"Have I ever listened to anything you told me to do or not

to do?"

That much was true, and Merrick realized there was little he could do to convince Alpin to keep his mouth shut.

When he turned back to his brother, Harmon was staring at him and Alpin. He arched a brow, and Merrick shook his head, hoping Harmon would get the hint.

Of course, he didn't, because fuck Merrick's life.

"And who is this? Your partner?"

Alpin beamed and pushed Merrick out of the way to get to Harmon. "Just a friend," he said, offering Harmon's hand. "For now. My name is Alpin."

Harmon shook, seemingly as happy as Alpin to meet him. Merrick would have to work hard to keep these two apart, although the reason they were here would probably be enough to wipe the smile off both their faces.

"Why don't you come in?" Harmon asked as he stepped aside.

The door revealed a courtyard. It was wide and long, with two other doors. One of them led into the tower, while the other went into the house proper. That was where Harmon led them, which was a relief. When Merrick had been a prisoner here, he'd been kept under the tower. Sigmund had known better than to try to stick him into the tower itself. It would have been too easy for Merrick to shift and fly away.

The house door opened into a small entrance. It looked the way it had when Merrick had lived here, but not exactly. It was still elegant and, as Alpin had mentioned, looked like it belonged in a castle, but it was more homey now, with a few umbrellas abandoned by the door and several pairs of boots. The sight of the common objects next to the finely decorated wooden bench and a colorful tapestry on the wall was odd but not unwelcome. It was good to see things truly had changed since Sigmund had died.

"You remember where Sigmund's office was," Harmon

murmured.

"Is that where we'll be talking?" Merrick asked.

"I thought it would be for the best. As much as I'd like to think you're here because you missed us, I doubt that's the case."

Merrick shouldn't feel guilty, but he did. After everything Harmon had done for him, he hadn't looked back when he'd left. They still communicated, but mostly through email and messages. He'd never planned on coming back, even though he knew how much Harmon cared about him. He realized how much of an asshole that made him, but he hadn't been sure he could deal with being here. He still wasn't.

"This place is awesome," Alpin said.

Harmon smiled at him. "I'm glad you enjoy it. We've tried making it more of a home in recent years."

"I think you managed. I mean, it's odd to see an abandoned mug on that clearly expensive table, but I like what you've done with the place."

Merrick did, too. Every step he took revealed more changes, and he could hardly believe this was the place where he'd been kept prisoner. Well, he'd been in the dungeon, but still. Several times, Sigmund had taken him out, wanting him to see what he could have if he finally gave in. Merrick never had, and back then, he'd been angry at the other vampires he could see living their lives. He hadn't realized that there was nothing any of them could do.

Except there was, and Harmon had done it.

Harmon led the way toward his office as if Merrick couldn't remember where it was. Merrick did his best to focus on the floor in front of him, because he didn't want to see things that might bring back bad memories. He didn't blame anyone for what had happened to him anymore, but he couldn't be sure all resentment was gone. The only vampire he'd kept in touch with was Harmon, and he wanted to keep things that way. He didn't need any more complications in his life, especially with Alpin already in it.

"It was a surprise to get your phone call," Harmon said.

"I should have called way sooner, but a lot has happened."

"His club went up in flames," Alpin not so helpfully explained.

Harmon turned wide eyes to Merrick. "What?"

"It's a long story. It's why we're here, so you'll get details soon."

"For some reason, I'm both eager to hear what you have to say and terrified," Harmon murmured.

Merrick shared that feeling. He didn't want anything to do with any of this, but unfortunately for him, he was right in the middle of it.

They walked through the ballroom with its chandeliers, black and white checkered floor, and many blindingly white columns. This was where Sigmund had enjoyed having meetings with the entire coven, usually to humiliate one or more members. It felt empty and slightly cold, as if the coven didn't use the room much. All of them probably had bad memories of this place.

Merrick couldn't avoid looking around, and he was glad to see more and more changes as they moved deeper into the castle. Most of the old, stuffy furniture was gone or, in some cases, had been reupholstered. The suits of armor still stood in the hallways, but someone had taken it upon themselves to decorate them. One was dressed like Santa Claus, while another had a witch's hat on top of its head. It made Merrick smile until he remembered that he didn't want Alpin to see him like that.

Finally, they reached what had been Sigmund's office. Harmon opened the door and waved them in, and Merrick steeled himself.

The room itself hadn't changed. The stone walls, wooden

floors, ceilings, and windows were the same. Everything else was different, though, and gone were the deer antlers and swords on the walls. The room was filled with dark furniture, soft-looking carpets, and new art on the walls. Harmon had made the place his, which Merrick was happy to see.

A big wooden desk stood in front of one of the windows. Harmon walked around it, gesturing at the chairs on the other side as he did so. "Please, sit down. I think it would be best to sit while we have this conversation because it doesn't sound like anything good."

Alpin snorted. "It's not."

"Can I offer you refreshments? We don't use live donors, but we do have blood available."

Merrick's mouth tasted like ashes at the reminder that no matter how many times he told himself he wasn't a vampire, he really was. He was lucky he could survive on human food, but sometimes, his vampire side wanted more. That was when he freaked out the worst and tried to put even more distance between himself and his past.

Alpin settled into one of the chairs. "Thank you, but I'm fine. I suspect Merrick is, too."

Harmon's smile was sad. "I believe you're right. He never took well to being a vampire."

Merrick chose to ignore that because it was his brother speaking and settled in the chair Alpin had left empty. Harmon sat on the other side of the desk and steepled his fingers together, staring at Merrick and Alpin. "Now, why don't you tell me what happened?"

It didn't take long for Merrick to explain everything that had been happening to Harmon. Harmon listened carefully, nodding and humming a few times. Alpin could tell he wanted to ask questions, but he didn't interrupt Merrick, which Alpin appreciated.

He looked around the office. Merrick had been hiding a whole bunch of things from everyone, and Alpin was dying to find out more. The coven seemed to be well established here, and the house was nice. It felt a bit like the house Alpin shared with his father and a few of his siblings—like a home. Why would Merrick want to stay away? Harmon was friendly, too, and both the brothers appeared happy to see the other. That probably meant Harmon had nothing to do with Merrick wanting to stay away.

So, it was because of their maker. That was the only thing that made sense, and Alpin wanted to ask, but he knew better than to ask Merrick. Usually, he wouldn't have cared about hurting Merrick's feelings, but this was anything but normal, at least for him. He didn't want to hurt Merrick, not even emotionally. It wasn't like him to care that much about someone who wasn't part of his family, which meant he'd finally had to admit, at least to himself, that he cared about Merrick.

Maybe even more than cared.

The thought was terrifying, mostly because Alpin didn't like feeling out of control. Even when he had a guy fuck him, he was always in control, and not only of his emotions. Things had been dangerous for men like him in the past, especially before he'd been turned into a vampire. He'd always been careful when he was with someone, even after he could have relaxed.

But he wanted to forget about everything that wasn't Merrick when he was with him. Hell, when they'd fucked at the club, the door had been open, and Alpin hadn't even noticed. Anyone could have walked in on them, and he hadn't cared. He'd been lost in Merrick, and he knew it would happen again if Merrick relaxed enough to give him a chance.

"Well, that sounds like a mess," Harmon said as he leaned back in his chair.

Merrick had stopped talking, so he was probably done with his explanation. Alpin was glad. It was getting late in the night because they'd had a late start to drive here, and they needed to get back on the road as soon as possible. It would mean more time alone with Merrick, and maybe Alpin would be able to ask some of the questions that burned his lips.

"It is," Merrick confirmed. "I hate that I brought all this trouble to the pack, but there's no changing that."

"You didn't do anything," Alpin said, glaring at Merrick. "The clan would have done this even without you and Arlen in the mix. They want power, and that means getting rid of the packs that could be a danger to them. Stop taking all the blame and look at things rationally."

Merrick glared right back as he got to his feet. "We should head back," he said, turning back to Harmon and effectively dismissing Alpin.

Alpin stuck his tongue out at Merrick's back because he felt petty and kind of hated him right now.

Dammit.

Harmon noticed and seemed amused, but as he opened his mouth to say something, a clashing thunder made the entire house vibrate. The sky outside opened, rain pouring down in sheets as lightning illuminated the night. The three of them peeked outside as the lightning struck a tree in the distance.

"It looks like you're not going anywhere," Harmon said. "I'll have a room prepared for you. Or two?"

Merrick didn't look amused. "Two. But it's just a little rain. We can make it back."

"Not before dawn, and while I know it's not a problem for you, it will be for Alpin."

Alpin wondered if Merrick would insist they do it anyway. He wouldn't put it past him. It wasn't like Alpin would go up in flames or anything like that, but he might get a bad sunburn, and that was never comfortable.

Merrick eyed Alpin as if he were weighing the pros and

cons of going. Alpin narrowed his eyes at him, hoping he was making it obvious that he was very much in the *stay here for the day* camp.

Merrick sighed, and his shoulders slumped. "Fine. We'll stay. And thank you for offering a bed."

Harmon smiled. "It's the least I can do. Besides, I'm glad to spend some time with you. It's been too long."

And that was the only reason why Alpin kept some distance between himself and Merrick over the next hour. They went downstairs to grab some blood, which Merrick declined, but Alpin happily took. He didn't fully understand why Merrick was so opposed to being a vampire, but since his turning sounded like it hadn't been consensual, maybe it made sense. Unlike Harmon, Merrick had a choice. He could survive on human food, so he could avoid blood. Harmon, on the other hand, had needed to make his peace with being a vampire. Alpin couldn't put himself in their place, because he'd known what he was getting into when he'd asked Tyrian to turn him.

"Here you go," Harmon said, standing in the middle of the hallway upstairs. "These two rooms are for you." He pointed at two doors. "I'll see you this evening."

Alpin waited until Harmon hugged Merrick and left before he turned to the dragon. Merrick had already opened one of the doors and was slipping through it. He was attempting to escape, wasn't he? It was adorable, but he should have known better.

Alpin wasn't about to waste this opportunity.

He slunk toward the still-open door and raised a hand to stop it from fully closing. Merrick glared at him, but there was no heat in his gaze.

"What are you doing?" he asked.

"I think you know."

Merrick rubbed his face. "Not right now, please. I'm tired."

"I am, too. I'm also tired of resisting this, and you can't tell me I'm the only one." Alpin pushed the door, and Merrick allowed him into the room. "We can stop acting like we don't want each other."

"What are you saying?" Merrick didn't sound opposed.

Alpin smiled. It wasn't his grin or his smirk. It was a genuine smile, because being with Merrick made him happy. "That I want you, and not just for sex. You're the most infuriating man I've ever met, but also the sexiest. You make pushing people away look like child's play, but you managed to wiggle your way into my heart in a way no one else has. I'm confused and, honestly, a bit weirded out, but I tried resisting, and it's useless." Alpin closed the door and leaned against it. "I'm ready to see what this can be. I'm not saying it'll be easy because, let's be real, nothing ever is with me, and adding you to the mix will only make it worse, but —"

Alpin didn't get to finish his sentence, because Merrick crushed their lips together, both of his arms going around Alpin's back. One hand lodged into Alpin's hair at the back of his head, keeping his face in place so Merrick could devour him.

And devour him, he did.

Alpin moaned and opened his mouth. He wanted more, and Merrick seemed intent on giving it to him.

He pushed his hands under Alpin's sweater, clearly knowing what he wanted because he aimed straight for Alpin's right nipple. Alpin shivered when Merrick's fingers skimmed it. He wanted Merrick's hands all over him, touching every inch of his body, but he could start with a nipple. He arched his back, allowing Merrick to push the sweater up. He bunched it under Alpin's arms, but the material felt heavy and too warm, and Alpin was already losing his patience.

He growled in displeasure and let go of Merrick's shoulders so he could get rid of the sweater. It was one of his favorites, but right now, he wanted it far away from his body because it was blocking Merrick's access.

Merrick chuckled and nipped at Alpin's lips before moving away. He'd understood what Alpin wanted without Alpin needing to say anything. Alpin took off the sweater and threw it to the floor, then stared at Merrick because how could he not?

Merrick had been sexy before, but now it was more than that. His cheeks were flushed and he was breathing hard, which made Alpin feel incredibly smug because it was because of him. He was the only one who could turn the stoic Merrick into this sexy, needy mess, and he was damn proud of that.

Merrick whipped his own sweater off and moved back to Alpin. He ran his fingers down Alpin's chest, making him shiver, never looking away from him as he aimed for Alpin's jeans. He dipped one fingertip under the button and played with the hair he found there, tugging none too gently until Alpin wanted to scream.

He needed more, dammit.

Alpin swallowed and nodded without hesitation. He wasn't even sure if Merrick was just being an asshole or if he was asking permission, but just in case, he wanted Merrick to know he had it.

His dick twitched in his jeans when Merrick finally popped open the button, then slowly lowered the zipper. He hooked his fingers under the waist of the jeans and the underwear and slowly pushed everything down, exposing Alpin's body with a slowness that made Alpin want to scream. He almost threw Merrick on the bed, but something stopped him.

The way Merrick touched him and continued staring at him felt special. Maybe it was. To Alpin, sex had only ever been sex, but so much more was happening right now. He had no idea what he was doing, and giving over control felt good, even though it was scary. The fact that Alpin trusted Merrick enough to do so was even scarier, but he didn't even hesitate.

Merrick was careful as he freed Alpin from his clothes, pushing them down his legs. He had to pause to take off Alpin's shoes and socks, but every time he touched Alpin, he felt cherished. He wasn't used to that, and by the time he stood naked in front of Merrick, he felt flustered and out of his depth.

He didn't try to shield his body from Merrick's sight, and Merrick took full advantage of it, staring at him without shame. He never looked away as he quickly finished undressing. There was much less care in the way he moved now, as if he didn't matter as much as Alpin.

Alpin was so flustered that he needed a moment. Merrick's gaze seemed to follow him as he moved away from the door and toward the bed. He paused by the nightstand, relieved to see a bottle of lube when he slid open the drawer. He took it out and hopped onto the bed, still avoiding looking at Merrick. He lay on the mattress and stretched, both because he felt like it and because he knew Merrick was looking.

He was. Alpin couldn't look away anymore when the mattress dipped and Merrick joined him. He settled between Alpin's spread legs, still only staring, but thankfully, that didn't last long.

Merrick leaned closer and pressed his palms against Alpin's thighs. He slid them up, finding a way to touch every single inch of the sensitive skin. Alpin licked his lips and stared as Merrick pressed a kiss to his inner thigh, so close to his cock, yet so far. He didn't have Alpin wait, though, which was good because Alpin might have started screaming if he had.

He wrapped his fingers around Alpin's, his lips moving into a smile against the skin of Alpin's thigh. Alpin narrowed his eyes at him, silently telling him to stop fucking around if he didn't want to find out what Alpin was ready to do in order to get him to fuck him.

Merrick smirked and settled more comfortably between Alpin's legs. Then he lowered his mouth and swallowed Alpin's cock.

It was everything Alpin had hoped it would be. Strangely, even though it definitely wasn't the first time someone sucked his cock, it felt different. Maybe it was because of the way Merrick held his gaze, or maybe it was because of the way he touched him as if he was precious and much more than just a cock to have fun with. Whatever the reason, it made Alpin's eyes prickle, and he wasn't about to start crying while getting the best blowjob of his life.

The best way for him to push all these feelings away was to get fucked, so he moved quickly, grabbing Merrick's shoulders and flipping their positions. He mourned the loss of Merrick's mouth on his dick, but he was about to get Merrick's cock in his ass, which would no doubt be just as good.

Merrick could have resisted, but he allowed Alpin to slam him to his back. He watched as Alpin grabbed the lube and straddled his lap, never once trying to stop or slow him down. Maybe Merrick wanted him as much as Alpin wanted him, or maybe he was uncomfortable with all these weird feelings, too.

Alpin didn't care.

He made quick work of prepping himself, shoving two slick fingers into his ass and moving them around. He didn't need or want more. Tomorrow night, when they were back on the road, he wanted to still feel Merrick inside of him.

Merrick's hands grabbed Alpin's hips as he moved into the right position. Alpin loved the way Merrick handled him — as if he were precious and maybe even fragile. They both knew he wasn't, but it was one of the reasons this was so different. No one had ever made Alpin feel the way Merrick did, and it didn't matter if Alpin was uncomfortable with all of this.

Well, except for the sex. *That* he was plenty comfortable with because he knew what he was doing.

But even the sex was different, wasn't it? Merrick made him feel like he was important and *loved*.

Alpin slicked Merrick's cock with the lube still on his hand, then held it up as he lowered himself onto it. Merrick tensed, but he didn't try to stop Alpin, which was a relief, because Alpin wasn't sure he'd have been able to.

Merrick was perfect in him. Alpin's ass stretched around him just so, almost too painful but oh so pleasurable. He'd definitely feel him tomorrow.

One look at Merrick, and Alpin's eyes prickled again. What the fuck was it with these feelings? Why couldn't they leave Alpin alone?

He pushed them away and pushed up on his knees, then bounced down. This was what he knew, what he was good at, and what he needed to focus on.

The sex was great, maybe even perfect. Merrick let Alpin do whatever he wanted and control the rhythm and how hard he fucked himself on his cock, which made Alpin feel less overwhelmed. He hadn't had to ask—he'd known what Alpin needed.

Merrick stared at Alpin with soft eyes the entire time, even when he finally started moving with him. He held Alpin when Alpin came, with such tenderness that Alpin almost did cry. He hadn't known Merrick was capable of this or that he'd needed it so badly.

But he *had* needed it, just like he needed it when Merrick gathered him into his arms after they both came, making him feel protected and like Merrick would never let him go, no matter how impossible it seemed to make things work.

CHAPTER FOUR

M errick should have known that sneaking out of bed wouldn't be as easy as it usually was when he had one-night stands. Alpin was like a barnacle, clinging onto him as if he were afraid Merrick would disappear. He wasn't wrong, since that was what Merrick was trying to do, but he was making it harder than it should be.

Merrick grabbed his pillow, pushed it between his body and Alpin's, and held his breath. He watched as Alpin smacked his lips, then snuggled against the pillow, happy and content. Leaving him like this wasn't something Merrick was proud of, but he hadn't been planning for anything to happen last night, and he had no idea how to deal with it. Right now, he should be at home, in his own bed, getting ready for breakfast. Instead, he'd woken up in Alpin's arms, and it had been much nicer than he could ever have expected.

He wasn't one for relationships. They complicated everything, and he had enough complications in his life. Alpin, especially, would be the worst person to have a relationship with considering the mess they all were in, along with his personality. He and Merrick clashed, and there was nothing they could do to change that.

Even though Merrick found himself wondering if maybe, he was wrong.

He shook his head and went to the bathroom. He moved as silently as possible, not wanting to wake Alpin. If Alpin opened his eyes, he'd have something to say about what happened. He'd probably demand an explanation, or maybe he'd declare the two of them were dating now. He hadn't struck Merrick as being a relationship kind of vampire, but things could change.

Clearly.

Merrick had the fastest shower he'd ever had, then peeked back into the bedroom. Alpin was still hugging the pillow, looking peaceful, and that was all Merrick wanted.

Really.

Merrick grabbed the clothes he'd been wearing yesterday since that was all he had, put them on — except for the underwear, which he pushed into his back pocket after folding it — and stepped out into the hallway. When he closed the door, he waited for a moment to see if the sound had awakened Alpin, but everything was silent in the bedroom. Relieved he'd managed to escape, Merrick made his way downstairs.

It was almost easy to ignore the house around him, because he couldn't stop thinking about Alpin. What did all of this mean? Neither Alpin nor Merrick did relationships, so why were they pulled toward each other so strongly? Why couldn't they stay away from each other, even though they both wanted to?

Merrick's stomach grumbled, and he picked up his pace. He remembered where the kitchen was. The problem was that he *hadn't* remembered that everyone in the house was a vampire, even after visiting the kitchen before going to bed, which meant that when he opened the fridge, it was full of blood bags. There was no food in sight, not even when, after inspecting the fridge, Merrick moved on to the cupboards.

What was he supposed to eat?

"You do realize you can survive on blood," someone drawled from behind him.

He couldn't help but smile at his brother's voice, even though he already disliked where the conversation was going. "I don't drink blood," he declared as he turned to face

Harmon.

Harmon was wearing a pair of sleep pants that looked like they might be silk. He'd thrown on a knitted sweater and had thick socks on his feet. That wasn't a bad idea considering how cold the house was. It had to be hell to heat.

Harmon sighed and stepped into the room. He ignored Merrick as he moved toward the fridge and grabbed one of the bags of blood. Merrick sat at the table, staring down at his hands so he wouldn't have to see what Harmon was doing. By the time Harmon was done and sitting in front of Merrick, he was sipping from a stainless-steel cup. Even the straw was steel, so there was no hint of blood.

Merrick relaxed. His brother wouldn't do anything to make him uncomfortable. He should have remembered that.

"You still don't drink blood," Harmon said.

And Merrick was angry again. "I don't want to."

"I realize that, but you're not just a dragon shifter. You have a vampire side, and I'd hoped you'd learned to live with it. You don't have to like it, but I truly believe that ignoring it will only bring trouble. Besides, unless you told the clan what happened to you, using your vampire side could be an asset in this war."

Merrick rubbed his face. He'd thought about that, but he wasn't sure he could bring himself to use the side he'd been forced to accept.

"I'm really sorry I couldn't do more for you," Harmon whispered.

There was pain in his gaze, and Merrick hated that he'd been the one who put it there. It wasn't his fault, but still. Harmon was his brother, and he didn't want him to hurt. "What happened to me was inevitable," he said slowly. "As soon as Sigmund saw me, my fate was sealed."

"I still should have done more."

"What more *could* you have done? You protected and fed

me. You stood up for me, and when I would have made myself this coven's leader, you stepped in. You dealt with Sigmund for me. You also gave me money." Harmon was the reason Merrick had been able to pay for half the club. The club wouldn't have existed if it hadn't been for him.

"That was Sigmund's money," Harmon said dismissively. "But I suppose we can both agree that we're sorry about what happened. I should have done more, and you should have visited more often or, at the very least, called. I've missed you. It's kind of bad that it's taken a war with the dragons for you to come back."

"You're right. I'm sorry I didn't come around sooner."

"Was coming here your idea, or did it come from Alpin?"

The smirk on Harmon's lips told Merrick he wanted to ask more questions. They'd stepped away from the seriousness of their past, but for the first time ever, Merrick kind of wished they could get back to it. He wouldn't hurt Harmon that way, so he forged ahead. "He's just a friend," he said.

"I suppose he could be, although, at the very least, he's a friend with benefits, from what I heard last night."

Merrick wasn't going to blush, dammit. "We're both adults."

"I never said you weren't, but you like him."

Merrick wouldn't ever admit to anyone else, least of all Alpin. "Yeah, I do," he told his brother.

"It's not a bad thing. I know you don't trust anyone but your closest friends and family, but maybe it's time to let someone in."

Merrick was glad when two women drifted into the kitchen, because it meant he didn't have to answer. It also meant he had to hug them and reassure them that he was all right when they threw themselves at him, but he was fine with that.

He hadn't realized how much the coven cared about him.

He certainly hadn't thought they'd miss him the way they seemed to have, and when, after Michelle and Rachel left the kitchen, Tarrant came in and reacted the way they had, it was easier to hug him.

Then Alpin ruined everything by coming in.

He arched a brow, and Merrick quickly let go of Tarrant.

"You replaced me so quickly," Alpin said with a teasing smile.

"I like having options," Merrick answered, his voice dry.

But that didn't stop Alpin. He grinned, then floundered closer to kiss Merrick's cheek. "As long as I'm your favorite."

Merrick rolled his eyes to hide his embarrassment, especially when he realized both Tarrant and Harmon were staring. Thankfully, Harmon took control and guided Alpin toward the fridge so he could have his breakfast. That allowed Merrick to sit back down and breathe, which he sorely needed after the day and evening he'd just had.

"I'm sorry you can't stay longer," Harmon said once it was clear the storm was over and Alpin and Merrick could head home. "And reassure everyone that the coven will help them with anything they need. This is our war, too, since you're involved."

His words made Merrick emotional, which he didn't like. Still, he owed a lot to Harmon. He also owed a lot to himself, including not losing the few family members he had. "I promise I'll visit soon."

"Will you keep that promise?"

"It might be complicated in the beginning considering what's happening with the clan, but I'm not staying away from you again. You're too important to me."

"I'm happy to hear that. Take care, Merrick." He hesitated. "And take care of Alpin. I know he's bubbly and happy, but there's more to him than what he allows you to see."

Merrick carried those words all the way back to the car. He

kept an eye on Alpin, and sure enough, as soon as they were alone, he got quiet. He stared out the window as Merrick drove them away, and Merrick let him be, even though he was curious.

What was going through Alpin's mind? Did it have something to do with what had happened last night between them, or was he already focused on what the clan would do next?

Alpin was quiet as he stared out the window. There was no way Merrick hadn't noticed, but thankfully, he didn't say anything about it. He was probably one of the few who wouldn't ask Alpin what was going on and why he wasn't talking.

Maybe it meant they belonged together or something like that. After yesterday, Alpin would have been ready to say yes, but after this evening, he wasn't sure. He'd been alone when he'd woken up, and he hadn't been surprised.

Merrick had been vulnerable. He'd allowed Alpin to see more than he usually showed anyone, and Alpin had expected him to freak out. The problem was that he didn't know if Merrick had gotten over it. Even if he had, what did it mean? Was it a one-night thing, or was Merrick ready for more?

It was impossible to know. They'd been poking at each other since they'd met, and Merrick had been pushing Alpin away since day one. The only way for Alpin to know what was going on would be to ask, but for the first time in his life, he was terrified to get an answer. Part of him wanted Merrick to say that of course it meant they were together now, but another part knew that wouldn't happen. He wasn't sure he was strong enough to face the pain that would come with that.

There was also the fact that Alpin was confused as hell. He shouldn't want a relationship. He'd never wanted one, not even with the cutest guys he'd had sex with. Why was

Merrick different?

In the beginning, Alpin believed that the only thing that made Merrick different was that he was a hybrid. He was a dragon shifter, yet he was also a vampire, and it was fascinating. Alpin wanted to find out more about him and what made him tick, and the fact that he was handsome and sexy only made him better. Now that he'd gotten to know Merrick, Alpin knew there was so much more to him than that. He was the entire package, something Alpin hadn't expected.

Merrick was a complicated man, like most people. He had likes and dislikes, and even though he'd never admit it, right now, he was at a vulnerable point in his life. He'd lost his home and his livelihood, and Alpin couldn't help but feel he was taking advantage. He'd forced himself on Merrick for this trip, so maybe he'd done the same last night. Merrick seemed eager to get Alpin in bed, but maybe Alpin had just seen what he wanted.

Once again, the only way to ensure what was happening would be to ask. When had words become so hard? And what did *Alpin* want?

Could he want a relationship?

He bit his lower lip and peeked at Merrick, who was focused on the road. His hands were wrapped around the steering wheel, and looking at them reminded Alpin of last night. Those hands had been on his body. They'd been on his skin, gentle yet strong, giving him pleasure and making him feel cherished. He hadn't expected that from Merrick, but maybe it hadn't been Merrick's doing.

Well, at least in part, it had been. Merrick could have made Alpin feel like he didn't matter, but he hadn't. Even though he found Alpin annoying, he'd made sure Alpin had everything he needed from what they'd done together.

Alpin closed his eyes. There was nothing more than trees and rocks to see outside, and he had some thinking to do. He needed to be honest with himself, and only then would he be able to decide what he wanted with Merrick.

Or at least, he hoped so.

So what did *he* want? He'd never been in a relationship, not even when he was human. He'd never felt the need for one, but he'd always known that eventually, he'd have one. He was a vampire and didn't want to spend eternity alone. Watching Mallory with Arlen had made him want more, but he'd tried convincing himself he didn't. Seeing how deeply in love Mallory and Arlen were was awe-inspiring, though, and Alpin couldn't help but wonder if he could have that with Merrick.

Maybe he needed to show Merrick they could be good together. He had no idea what he was doing when it came to relationships, but he suspected Merrick didn't, either. Of course, Merrick could say no and tell Alpin to fuck off. He probably would, knowing him. Besides, now was probably the worst moment for them to get together, considering the clan and the club.

But nothing about that stopped Alpin from wanting Merrick.

Alpin snapped his eyes open. The night was dark, but it didn't scare him like it had when he was a child. He was a creature of the night, a vampire, and being one had given him the time and opportunity to find out more about himself. So what if he'd never been a relationship guy? People changed, even people who lived forever — maybe especially them. Having so much time gave them the opportunity to be and do whatever they wanted, and Alpin wanted Merrick. Could it be as simple as that?

He looked sideways at Merrick. Merrick's attention was still on the road, and he was tapping his fingertips on the steering wheel even though they hadn't put music on. The rhythm seemed to be in his mind, and he was focused, so he didn't notice Alpin staring.

He was endearing.

In the beginning, Alpin only wanted sex from Merrick. Now, things were different, and while it was scary, that didn't mean it was a bad thing. Alpin was convinced of that, and he'd try to make Merrick see things his way. Having to convince Merrick they'd be good together wasn't the part that scared him. He was stubborn and had all the time in the world to make it happen.

He just hoped he wouldn't have to wait decades.

He'd always been impatient, but maybe he'd have to learn to deal in this situation. He wasn't the only one involved and didn't want to hurt Merrick. He didn't want *anyone* to be hurt.

Alpin would need to find the perfect moment to talk to Merrick, but he didn't think tonight was that moment. They were both tired and out of sorts and needed some rest and time away from each other before anything else. That way, they could relax and wrap their minds around what had happened between them.

Alpin's phone beeped in his pocket, and he wiggled until he was able to get it out of his jeans. He was surprised to see Kieran's name on the screen, then instantly worried.

"It's Kieran," he said, unlocking his phone.

"Has something happened?"

That was Alpin's fear, and clearly, Merrick shared it.

Alpin's shoulders slumped in relief when he saw what Kieran was asking. "No. He just wants to know if we feel up for patrolling tonight." Alpin had thought he was headed home, and he couldn't wait to shower again and put on clean clothes, but it would have to wait. He wasn't about to pitch a fit because he was being asked to do something he'd agreed to.

Merrick grunted. "I'm fine with it. If you'd rather go home, I can do it on my own."

"We're a team."

"Not because we wanted to be."

Alpin frowned. Did Merrick really have to make it sound like they were forced to work together? They were, but Alpin didn't find it unpleasant, yet Merrick always pointed out that they'd both rather not spend time together. "But we agreed to it. It's both our jobs, not only yours. You don't have to sound like you'd rather resuscitate your creator than work with me."

"That's not what I said."

"It was implied."

Merrick was glaring, so Alpin expected him to snap. He was surprised when instead, Merrick sucked in a breath. "I apologize. I guess we're both tense, which would explain why we're still sniping at each other."

"Everyone is tense." And what had happened last night, along with the fact that neither of them knew what was going on, wasn't helping.

Alpin sighed. Maybe he'd have to talk to Merrick sooner than he'd expected. That would be better than keeping on wondering what was happening between them and if they could be together. Alpin knew himself, and he had problems focusing on the best of days. The pack needed him to keep them safe, which meant he had to be fully in the game.

But he was afraid. For the first time, he was too afraid to ask a question.

And he didn't know what to do about that fear, how to conquer it, or even if he could. He didn't have many options. Either he talked to Merrick and found out what was happening between them and if there could be more than a one-night stand, or he kept his mouth shut and possibly lost whatever chance he had with Merrick. He knew what he wanted.

He just wasn't sure what he'd find the courage to do.

Merrick was relieved when, once they got closer to pack territory, Alpin started chatting again. It had been odd to be with him in the car without hearing his voice, and Merrick had no idea what to think about it. It was good to see Alpin was getting over whatever funk he'd been in, and hopefully, it meant they wouldn't have to give explanations to anyone waiting for them.

It was also good that they seemed to have a job to do tonight. Merrick couldn't go home and obsess over what he and Alpin had done, which was what he wanted to avoid. Everything was confused, and he felt that if he tried to focus on too many things at once, he'd go nuts. It was better if they kept busy, and that was what he intended to do.

"What do you think?" Alpin suddenly asked.

Merrick frowned, wondering what he'd been talking about. He'd tuned him out because it seemed Alpin was using a lot of words but not saying many things. He was filling the silence, which wasn't a surprise, considering the tension in the car. "I wasn't listening to you."

Alpin was silent for a moment before he burst out laughing. "Well, at least you're honest."

"I always try to be. I don't see a good reason to lie to people."

"How about if you don't want to hurt them?"

"Why would honesty hurt them?"

Alpin shrugged. "It can happen. Look at me. It hurts when people tell me to fuck off and that I'm too much for them."

"No one would dare do anything like that." Alpin was too adorable to hurt that way.

"I seem to remember a certain dragon shifter doing exactly that," Alpin said, but it was obvious from his tone that he was teasing.

Except he was right. Merrick *had* been blunt with him, and he knew it had hurt. He hadn't meant to do that, but he'd wanted Alpin to leave him alone.

It hadn't worked.

Even when hurt by Merrick's words, Alpin had pushed and pushed, and he was still right next to Merrick. He didn't give up, and while Merrick would never say that out loud to him, it was awe-inspiring. Alpin was stubborn and always seemed to know what he was doing. Merrick had his life in hand before, but since the club had burned down, he felt at a loss. He had no idea what to do with his life or how to deal with anything that was happening. He was ready to fight the clan, but what did that leave him? What could he do about the club and everything else? He was used to working every day, not having to think too much about things, but now his life was different. He was focused on different things and had many more people there with him. Alpin was one of those people, and as infuriating and annoying as he was, Merrick couldn't imagine his life without him.

And he had no clue what to do about that.

He was torn between enjoying Alpin's voice and his enthusiasm as he chatted and wanting to strangle him because he was never silent. It became even worse when Merrick realized Alpin was talking about his conquests.

"This one time, this guy did something with his tongue. I was never able to find anyone else able to do it."

Merrick grunted. "Do you really have to tell me about your exes?"

Alpin shrugged. "They're not my exes. They're just guys I slept with. And why shouldn't I tell you about them? Are you jealous?"

"Why would I be jealous?"

"It's okay if you are, you know? It's okay if I mean something to you."

But Merrick wasn't sure he was ready to admit that, least of all to Alpin. He was incredibly confused, and what Alpin was saying wasn't helping. "Can you please shut up?" he snapped.

Miraculously, Alpin did. The problem was that now Merrick felt guilty. He shouldn't have talked that way to Alpin, who was only making conversation and had to be as confused as Merrick was about what happened between them. Even if it had only been a joke for him, he didn't deserve for Merrick to talk to him like that.

Merrick took a deep breath. "I apologize."

"I'm almost afraid to ask what you're apologizing for," Alpin said.

"Snapping at you. I know it's not an excuse, but I'm worried about the clan, and now that I pulled my brother into this, I'm worried about him, too. He's one of the few people I care about in the world, and I'd never forgive myself if something happened to him and I was the cause of it."

"But you wouldn't be the cause of it. I mean, if something did happen to him, and I don't think it will, it would be because of the clan, not because of you. They're the ones who want a war."

"They are, but I still feel guilty. Harmon has a good life. I'm not sure it's what he wanted, but it's what he has, and he's made the best of it. You saw the house and how the coven members are with him. They love him, and they love each other. I don't want to destroy that just because the clan decided that Arlen and I shouldn't be allowed to have anything away from them."

"I'm not sure that's what they're aiming for. I mean, it looks like they're trying to destroy the entire supernatural community around them. They want supremacy."

Alpin wasn't wrong. The clan firmly believed that dragons were superior to any other supernatural creature, which meant they should be in charge. They wanted control, and while they were able to intimidate most other creatures, Arlen and Merrick knew who they were and what they did. They'd been standing up to the clan since they'd left, and Merrick had known their old clan leader wouldn't be happy about that. He had other things to focus on, but now, with the war with the pack brewing and Arlen and Merrick stuck in the middle, he'd finally turned his attention to them.

And he'd apparently decided to burn down their lives.

Merrick was relieved when they finally reached pack territory. He still had no idea what was happening between him and Alpin, but it would be good for them to focus on something else and give each other some time to deal with their feelings and thoughts. Maybe by the time they could go home, they'd both know more about what they wanted and what they were ready for, and if they didn't, well, they'd have to deal with it anyway. They wouldn't be able to ignore all of this for long, but Merrick was happy to do it for a little while longer.

They didn't go to Kieran's house when they got to pack territory. They had work to do and were both eager to do it. Merrick would have rather done it with someone else, but it seemed that life had decided he was stuck with Alpin, and he'd have to make his peace with that.

"Why don't you tell me about the clan?" Alpin said after a while. "I mean, I'm curious. I've never met dragons before, and I don't know much about you guys. I wouldn't want to do something stupid, you know? Although, of course, some people think that I say something stupid every time I open my mouth. I'm not sure there's much I can do about it if that's the case."

Merrick had parked the car in front of the house he shared with Arlen and Mallory, but they hadn't gone in, even though the lights were on. Instead, they'd headed straight to the forest without talking. They'd reached the area Kieran had assigned to them and had started walking the perimeter and listening to the sounds of the forest.

Merrick groaned. "Are you allergic to silence?"

Alpin grinned at him. "Maybe. Is that a problem?"

"Most people would have a problem with you not being able to keep your mouth shut."

"Are *you* one of those people?"

Merrick opened his mouth to answer, but a movement between the trees caught his attention. It was dark, so it was hard to see much, but he was pretty sure someone was there.

He opened his mouth to tell Alpin there was an intruder, but it was too late. A group of three wolves burst between the trees, headed straight for them. Alpin cried out, and Merrick was worried enough to look at him. He was relieved to see Alpin was in a defensive position, but he wasn't a fighter, no matter what he said. He could defend himself well enough, but they weren't facing just any enemy. This was a pack of wolves, and from the way they were running at them, they were bent on hurting them.

Alpin stared at the three wolves running toward him and Merrick for way too long. He had to react, but while his mind knew that, his body didn't seem to have gotten the memo.

He knew how to do this. He reminded himself of the many times he and his siblings had fought, trying to teach each other how to defend themselves. Alpin had always been the smallest, but it didn't mean he was useless and that he couldn't do this.

He swallowed as the first wolf reached him and Merrick. He'd expected Merrick to step forward and take charge, and he hadn't been wrong. Merrick threw himself forward, a snarl escaping his throat. The problem was that there were three wolves, and the two others focused on Alpin.

He flashed them a grin, making sure to expose his fangs.

Now that the shock was fading, he felt more in charge and wasn't afraid.

Much.

He grabbed the first wolf by the throat when they reached him. Most of the stories humans believed about vampires weren't true. They weren't super strong, and they could go out in the sun, although they were sensitive to it, so they tended not to do it. They were just a bit faster than a normal human, but Alpin had been trained to use that speed. He also trained regularly, so while his muscles strained as he raised the wolf, he managed to throw them against the closest tree.

Then the other wolf launched themselves at him.

The impact made the air whoosh out of Alpin's lungs. His vision went black, but only for a second. Still, by the time he could see again, the wolf was aiming for his throat. Alpin threw up his arms, expecting pain, but it was the only thing he could do. He needed to protect his throat.

Fangs sank into his arm, and he cried out. He used his other hand to push the wolf away, but the asshole clung on, and Alpin was afraid of tearing the flesh of his arm out. He could taste blood and was terrified, but he needed to fight.

He raised his free hand again and poked the wolf in the eyes with two fingers. The wolf whimpered and jerked away, giving Alpin time to scramble to his feet. He quickly looked around, expecting the first wolf to attack him again, but that one was busy with Merrick. The wolf Merrick had attacked in the beginning was on the ground, whimpering.

That left Alpin with just one wolf.

He held his arm against his chest as they circled each other. He didn't have much to defend himself, especially with one arm out. He had fangs, but it would be impossible for him to bite the wolf with all that fur. On the other hand, the wolf wouldn't find much resistance if they attempted to tear out Alpin's throat.

And they looked like they were going to try.

The wolf launched themselves at Alpin again. He tried to step away but stumbled on a root, and his back slammed against a tree. He rolled away as the wolf lunged, grinning when the wolf's muzzle hit the tree.

But the wolf wasn't done. They never stopped moving, and Alpin wasn't fast enough. The wolf grabbed his arm, the good one this time. The wolf pulled, and Alpin stumbled, tilting forward. That was when the wolf let go and reached for Alpin's throat.

Alpin raised his arms as he fell. He also tried to roll sideways so he'd end up on his back and hopefully would be able to get back to his feet quickly, but the wolf was attacking again. They tore through Alpin's arm, and Alpin reacted instinctively, pushing them away and trying to tuck himself into a ball. It wasn't tight enough. He felt the wolf's teeth sink into the flesh of his neck. It wasn't right in his throat, but rather sideways, but it was still enough to do damage that would end Alpin's life.

Warm blood spurted from the wounds created by the wolf's teeth. Alpin attempted to push the wolf away again, but he was getting weak and knew the end was near. He'd never thought this would happen. He hadn't had a reason to truly fight before, and here he was, dying the first time it presented itself. Merrick would probably have a good laugh when he realized what had happened, and Alpin couldn't even berate him for that. He'd been an idiot. He'd thought he could do this, and maybe he could have in other circumstances, but it was too late.

A roar made everything around them shake—the dirt under Alpin, the trees surrounding him, his entire body. The wolf's body tensed, then released, and Alpin felt their teeth withdraw from his throat. He wasn't sure why, but he expected the wolf to try to kill him from a better angle, so he steeled himself for what was coming.

The wolf was snatched away.

Alpin blinked, trying to understand what was happening and what he was seeing. The wolf had been there one second and gone the next, and from the whimpers he could hear, it was nothing good. He tried to sit up, but the only thing he could do was fully roll onto his back. His entire body hurt, but it didn't make sense. Only his arms and throat had been wounded.

He reached up with the arm that hurt less, touching his throat. His fingers were slick, but he couldn't tell if it was sweat or something else. Probably blood, if he was honest with himself.

He couldn't think. His mind was fuzzy, but he blinked his eyes open. He hadn't realized he'd closed them.

He didn't want to die in the darkness. If these were his last moments, he wanted to go staring at the sky. He'd always enjoyed the night sky more than the sky during the day, which was one of the reasons he hadn't hesitated when Tyrian had offered to turn him. The other reason was that he'd already been dying.

So he stared at the moon until something massive stepped in front of it. He blinked and tried to frown, but he wasn't sure he could control his expression anymore. His entire body was unresponsive, including the muscles in his forehead.

A huge head leaned toward him. It took him a moment to recognize it, and when he did, he gasped.

Merrick had shifted.

Even though it was dark, this was the moment of the day in which Alpin belonged. He could see perfectly, so he knew how beautiful Merrick was. His dragon body was massive but also graceful as he moved. Alpin wasn't afraid when Merrick reached for him with a dragon paw, gently touching his chest.

He wasn't afraid, but it didn't mean it didn't hurt.

He forced himself to smile. "Looks like we'll never find out if we would have worked as a couple," he whispered.

Merrick's eyes narrowed as if he were telling Alpin to shut the fuck up. He probably was, knowing him, and Alpin realized he was happy that he could predict what Merrick was thinking. He'd never know if they'd have worked out, but he could die believing they would have. He just hoped Merrick hadn't gotten too attached. He didn't want the dragon to isolate himself again. Merrick deserved love, and if he couldn't have it with Alpin, then Alpin wanted him to have it with someone else. As long as that person treated Merrick right, Alpin was fine with him moving on.

Merrick leaned back, then moved again. Alpin's eyes widened when he realized Merrick was trying to slide his paw under him, and he wasn't sure it was a good idea. "That's going to hurt," he said. His voice was nothing more than a whisper by now. "You don't need to do this. There's no way I can survive." Alpin was cold, and his body wasn't responding. He didn't have long, and he was sure Merrick knew that. "Go get the others. Tell them what happened and how brave I was, defending the pack."

Merrick rolled his eyes, which made Alpin laugh, or at least, he tried to. With the way his body hurt, the only sound that came out was a groan.

Merrick narrowed his eyes, then pushed his paw under Alpin harder. He had to help with his other paw, but he was incredibly gentle as he wrapped big fingers tipped with claws around Alpin's body. Once he had Alpin, he lifted him, and Alpin had to bite his lower lip so he wouldn't scream.

Merrick was doing what he could to make sure Alpin survived. Alpin was pretty sure it was useless, but if it made Merrick feel better, he'd go along with it.

He didn't have anything to lose anyway.

CHAPTER FIVE

Merrick normally wouldn't have moved Alpin, considering how much blood he was losing, but there wasn't a better option. They were deep in the forest, and he didn't think anyone had realized what had happened. He couldn't hear anyone coming closer to help them, and while he'd hesitated to shift into his dragon form before, he should have done so from the beginning. If he had, Alpin would be fine now. Instead, he was dying, and Merrick wasn't ready to face a world without Alpin in it.

So, moving as slowly and gently as he could, he picked up Alpin from the ground and cradled him to his chest. He didn't care about the dead wolves. He only cared about Alpin, and as he pushed into the air, he told himself that Alpin would be fine.

He was a vampire. Surely, his body could withstand much more damage than a human's. But the amount of blood he'd lost was terrifying. Even though Merrick couldn't see color as well in the darkness, he'd noticed the pool of dark stickiness Alpin had been lying in.

Merrick wanted to shift, to hold Alpin as a human, and to tell him everything would be all right. He wanted to tell Alpin that he cared about him and that once this madness was over, he wanted them to try to be together. What had happened when they were at the coven was only the first step in their relationship, and Merrick couldn't wait to find out how Alpin would change his life.

But he might never get to see that. If Alpin died before

Merrick could talk to him, before he could enjoy his life, Merrick would never forgive himself.

He'd fought as quickly as he could, but he should have been faster. He should have shifted right away.

But he couldn't focus on that when Alpin was dying in his arms. He was in his dragon form now, so he used it, crashing through the trees on his way up in the air. For a moment, he hesitated, unsure where he should go. Alpin trusted his family like he trusted no one else, and hopefully, Tyrian would know what to do. From the way both Alpin and his siblings talked about him, he seemed to have been taking care of them for a long time.

It only took a minute or so for Merrick to get there. He landed in front of the house, his weight shaking the ground under him. The lights were on, but no one came to see what was happening, so Merrick roared.

That would get their attention.

As soon as all his feet were on the ground, he shifted back to his human form. He cradled Alpin into his arms and rushed toward the house, and he almost sobbed when the door opened before he could get there. Tyrian stood in the entrance, peering out, his eyes widening when he saw Merrick.

"What happened?" he asked, running forward.

More people were coming out of the house. Merrick turned his attention to Tyrian since he needed to answer him. Someone tried to get Alpin from him, and he growled at them until he realized it was one of Alpin's brothers. Rex stared for a moment before Merrick nodded at him. He nodded back, then gently took Alpin.

"Merrick, what happened?" Tyrian snapped.

Merrick swallowed. "We were on patrol. Kieran called and asked us if we were willing to do it tonight. We both agreed, so we headed there right away. Three wolves attacked us. I killed all of them, but not before they hurt Alpin."

Tyrian nodded and turned toward the house, intent on following Rex. Merrick went after him, but Tyrian turned around, pressing a hand against his chest. "You're not coming in," he ordered.

"I need to make sure he's all right."

"You should have done that before he got hurt."

The words were almost a physical blow. Merrick staggered back, but he was angry, and he tended not to think before he reacted when that happened. He lunged forward, wanting to hurt Tyrian even though he knew the vampire was right.

Strong arms wrapped around his waist, pulling him back. He snarled, but they didn't let go, and when Merrick turned around, he saw it was another one of Alpin's brothers, Meyer. He didn't want to hurt anyone, especially not Alpin's siblings, so he sucked in a breath and tried to calm himself.

"Alpin agreed to go on patrol. He knew what he was doing. He knew he could be hurt," Merrick told Tyrian.

"I told him it was a bad idea for him to get involved, and I was right. I have to focus on helping him. The last thing I need is for you to mess things up, so you have to go."

"I care about him. I just want to make sure he's all right," Merrick protested.

"You've hated him since day one," Tyrian yelled. "I wouldn't be surprised if you'd stepped back and allowed the wolves to hurt him on purpose."

Merrick almost shifted right there and then. It had been a long time since he'd shifted without meaning to, and that had been back when he was a teenager. Tyrian made him angry enough for it to happen today, though.

But Alpin wouldn't want him to do this. Alpin would want him to think, and when he did, Merrick realized that Tyrian was terrified for the man he considered one of his sons.

Still, that didn't stop him from getting right into Tyrian's face. "I'd never do anything like that, especially to Alpin. I might not have liked him in the beginning, but things changed between us. I'm in love with him, and he's in love with me." Or at least, Merrick thought that was the case. "He's the only one who has a right to tell me to stay away."

"I don't care. I need to be able to focus to make sure he lives, and having you hovering over my shoulder won't allow me to do that. You have to go." Tyrian pushed Merrick back.

Merrick had to resist the urge to snap his teeth at him, even though they were human at the moment. He felt the need to bite Tyrian, even though Tyrian was only thinking about Alpin and how to save him.

"I'll call Arlen and Mallory," Meyer whispered.

Merrick wanted to rage, to tell Tyrian he had nothing to do with this, but could he? He'd done what he could, fighting the wolves, but he'd shifted too late. He could have saved Alpin a lot of pain and probably saved him from death if he hadn't hesitated.

And now he might lose the only man who'd interested him enough to make him want to see if they could be together.

Meyer pulled at him again, and this time, Merrick allowed himself to be guided away. He didn't even move toward the house when Meyer let him go to get his phone out. Instead, he watched Tyrian rush inside and prayed.

He didn't know how much time had passed when a hand grabbed his shoulder. He jerked back, ready to defend himself, relaxing only when he saw it was Arlen. Arlen raised both his hands as if he feared Merrick, which made Merrick feel like a dick.

"What happened?" Arlen asked.

"It was my fault," Merrick whispered. "I didn't want to shift because I didn't want to risk hurting Alpin along with the wolves."

"You did what was right. I'm sure Alpin will agree once he's better."

A sob escaped Merrick's lips, so he pressed them together. "What if he doesn't get better?"

Arlen wrapped an arm around Merrick's shoulders. "He will. That's what you have to focus on. It's what we *all* have to focus on. Now, why don't you let me take you home? You need clothes, if anything, because no one wants to have to stare at your naked ass."

Merrick chuckled, but it quickly transformed into another sob. He rubbed his face with both his hands. He was exhausted, and not just because of the fight. He needed rest and food if he wanted to be there when Alpin woke up. That meant he had to allow Arlen to take him back to the home they shared.

"I need to know that Alpin is all right before I go," he said.

"Mallory's staying here with the others. He'll let me know as soon as something happens," Arlen promised.

Merrick could only hope Mallory would do just that and that he wouldn't blame him for what happened. Merrick had been angry at Tyrian's words, but he'd been the first to blame himself, so was it a surprise that Alpin's father had done the same?

"Let's go home," Arlen whispered.

Merrick allowed his best friend, his *brother*, to lead him away. He was leaving his heart behind, but there was nothing he could do for the moment.

How could it come to this? Why had it taken Alpin almost dying, possibly dying still, for Merrick to realize how much he cared about him?

Alpin was in pain.

He could hear people around him, whispering and touching him, moving him this way and that, and he tried to push them away because they made the pain worse, but he was too weak. He couldn't quite remember what he'd done to feel this way, but sometimes he had flashes of a wolf throwing itself at him, and it was terrifying.

The pain reached its peak when someone touched Alpin's throat. He cried out and tried to get away, but two strong hands pinned him down. Then, something small and hard pressed against his lips, and his upper body was lifted.

He felt like a doll, being moved and touched without being able to react beyond a few moans. He wanted to resist, but the faint scent of blood reached his nostrils. He sucked in a breath, and the hold on his shoulders softened.

"Drink," a voice ordered.

Alpin wouldn't have been able to resist even if he'd wanted to. His body craved the blood, so he gave in, wrapping his lips around what he now realized was a metal straw. He sucked, and when the blood hit his tongue, it was the best thing he'd ever tasted. He continued sucking, sending down mouthfuls of blood so quickly that some of it dribbled down his chin. His body seemed to need it, because it greedily demanded more, even when nothing else came in through the straw.

"I'll give you more in a little while," the same voice said.

Alpin now recognized it as Tyrian's, and he tried to open his eyes, but he felt too tired to even do that. Still, he tried again, but Tyrian gently touched his forehead.

"Sleep," he ordered. "Your body needs it, and everything will still be here when you wake up. The wound on your throat is already healing, thanks to the blood, but I'll keep an eye on it. I'll make sure nothing else happens to you, at least tonight. You're safe."

Alpin believed him. He always believed Tyrian, who'd saved him from certain death when he was still human. It seemed he'd also saved him from certain death now that he was a vampire, and Alpin wasn't sure how to feel about owing him so much.

Maybe it didn't matter. Tyrian was his father, or at least, that was how Alpin saw him. He'd known he was safe as soon as he'd heard Tyrian's voice. Now that Tyrian had reassured him, it was easier to give in to sleep. It was pulling at Alpin's body, drawing him deep, and he let go.

Whatever was happening in the world around him, Tyrian would keep them safe.

The next time Alpin returned to consciousness, he felt both better and worse. The pain was still there, almost as if he hadn't been healing, but then, drinking blood wouldn't work miracles. It would take him some time to get better, and the fact that he'd survived was a miracle.

He blinked his eyes open. They were the only things he could move without being in pain, so he took advantage of that and looked around. He recognized the room that had been his since he and his family had arrived in pack territory, and he relaxed, knowing he was home. It meant it was safe and that Tyrian and the others were probably somewhere around, waiting for him to wake up.

He had. He'd survived, even though he hadn't been sure he would. Hell, he'd been convinced he'd die, and he vaguely remembered telling Merrick to let him go.

Alpin tried sitting up at the thought of Merrick. Where was the dragon shifter? Why wasn't he here, holding Alpin's hand? Alpin felt he deserved it after what had happened to him.

But he and Merrick hadn't talked about what came next for them. They hadn't had the opportunity, and maybe Merrick had decided this would be the perfect moment to vanish from Alpin's life. Alpin didn't want to believe it, but he didn't know Merrick that well.

He reached up, touching his throat. It was heavily bandaged, and even touching it through all of that made it hurt.

He dropped his hands and told himself he wouldn't do that again, especially when a flash of pain shot through his arm. Right, he'd been bitten there, too.

So, he was in pain, not fully healed, and alone. How had that happened? Was Merrick still out there, fighting to protect the pack? There had only been three wolves, but there could easily have been more. Maybe they'd been hiding in the forest, waiting until the first three took care of Merrick and Alpin. Maybe they'd taken over the pack while Alpin was sleeping, although he doubted they had. He wouldn't be here, still alive and relatively comfortable.

He licked his lips. His throat was parched, but thankfully, there was a stainless-steel tumbler on the nightstand. There was a metal straw in it, so it would be easier for Alpin to drink. He reached out, but he couldn't quite touch the tumbler, which meant he'd have to move.

He stared at the ceiling for a moment. He supposed he might as well start now. He wanted to get to Merrick, anyway. The sooner he did, the sooner he'd get an explanation as to what had happened and why Merrick wasn't here.

Alpin's body didn't just hurt. It was stiff, and he might have wondered how much time he'd been in bed if he hadn't been wounded. He wasn't healed yet, so it couldn't be that long.

With a lot of help from the edge of the bed and a few pillows, Alpin managed to pull himself into a sitting position. By the time his back was against the headboard, he was breathing hard, and he wondered if the wound on his neck had reopened. It felt damp under the bandages, which couldn't be good.

That was when the bedroom door opened. Tyrian came in, clearly lost in his thoughts because he froze when he saw Alpin. For a moment, they stared at each other. Then Tyrian rushed toward the bed. He reached for Alpin but seemed to think better of it and dropped his hands. Alpin was grateful. He wanted a hug, but he suspected it would hurt.

"Hey," he whispered. He was happy to find out his voice still worked. He hadn't been entirely sure, considering his throat had been bitten into.

"What were you trying to do?" Tyrian asked.

Alpin gestured at the tumbler. Tyrian took it and held it up to Alpin's lips, and Alpin eagerly took a sip. The blood was warm and fresh, and it tasted like heaven. He drank a bit more, then leaned back and watched as Tyrian put away the tumbler.

"What happened to me?" Alpin asked.

Tyrian's expression was pinched. "What do you think happened?"

"Well, I remember a wolf trying to tear my throat out." That wasn't the only thing that had happened. Alpin's arm hurt, too, and he hadn't been surprised to see it was bandaged.

Tyrian nodded. "You remember right. Three wolves attacked you and Merrick. They did quite a number on you, but Merrick got you here in time."

Tyrian seemed displeased, but it couldn't be because Alpin was alive. That meant something else was happening, and that something else might have to do with Merrick. "Where is he?" Alpin asked, even though he was afraid of the answer.

He was half convinced Merrick had decided he was too much of a bother. After all, they'd only had one day together. It had been good, but then Alpin had the brilliant idea of getting his throat torn out, and now he was stuck in bed in pain and unable to move. It wasn't great fun, so definitely not what Merrick would have expected from being with him.

"Don't worry about him. He's fine," Tyrian reassured him.

That didn't tell Alpin where Merrick was, although he supposed he was probably out there, getting rid of the bodies of the wolves they'd killed and being all handsome while doing it. Alpin wanted to go there and see, but he suspected he'd be stuck in bed for a while.

Just his luck, dammit.

"Whose blood is this?" he asked. It could be from the blood bank, but it tasted fresh.

That was surprising, since they lived with a wolf pack, but Tyrian confirmed Alpin was right. "Several of the wolves volunteered to give blood for you. This comes from a guy named Ollis."

Alpin remembered him. "Can you thank him for me?"

"Of course. You'll be able to thank him yourself, though."

"As soon as I'm out of bed, I will." Alpin's eyelids were heavy, but he didn't want to go to sleep. "I want to see Merrick."

"You will. You need more rest for now."

"I'd sleep better if Merrick was here."

"You'll have to make do," Tyrian murmured.

His tone made Alpin frown. Had something happened to Merrick? Something in Tyrian's voice made him worry, but before he could get a handle on his thoughts, darkness swallowed him as he lost his fight with his eyelids.

Merrick was going nuts. He needed to see Alpin and reassure himself that the vampire was fine, but how could he do that when he was being kept away? Every time he tried to leave, Arlen appeared and pulled him back. It was infuriating, and it needed to stop.

He was making a go at the front door again when someone knocked. Merrick froze, wondering if someone had found him out, especially when Arlen arrived from the living room and glared at him. "Where were you going?" Arlen asked.

"To see Alpin. What do you think?"

Arlen shook his head as he opened the door. "I don't want you going there. You almost fought with Tyrian."

"That wasn't my fault," Merrick muttered.

"I never said it was, but do you really want to fight with Mallory and Alpin's father?"

Kieran stood on the other side of the door, his head cocked as he listened to the conversation he'd walked in on. Merrick huffed. Of course he didn't want to fight with Mallory and Alpin's father. The man was taking care of Alpin and healing him.

But did he really have to keep Merrick away from Alpin? He didn't have a good reason to do so. Merrick hadn't been the one who harmed Alpin, and he certainly hadn't set him up to be hurt, no matter what Tyrian believed.

"I can come back later," Kieran said.

Arlen shook his head. "Come in."

Kieran did, his focus turning from Arlen to Merrick. Merrick wanted nothing more than to head out and to Alpin, but it seemed he'd have to wait again. Maybe it was for the best, or maybe not. He'd find out eventually.

But it was hard to focus on anything that wasn't Alpin. Mallory had sent word that Alpin was alive and recuperating already, and Tyrian had seemingly promised he'd be fine. Merrick had no reason not to believe him, in spite of the words they'd exchanged. He still needed to see Alpin with his own two eyes, which he wouldn't be able to do as long as he was stuck here.

"How are you feeling?" Kieran asked Merrick.

Arlen gestured toward the living room, and when Kieran followed him there, Merrick was forced to do the same. He gritted his teeth and reminded himself that Kieran had been nothing but good to him and Arlen. He needed to know what was happening so he'd be able to keep his pack safe, which was no doubt why he was here.

"I'm fine. I wasn't the one who got injured in the fight."

Kieran nodded. "That was Alpin. I'm glad to hear that he's doing all right."

"That's what I was told, too."

"I'm surprised you're not with him right now."

Merrick glared at Arlen. "I would be if some people weren't conspiring to keep me away." He looked at Kieran. "Tyrian believes I let Alpin get be hurt because I hate him."

Arlen tsked. "You know he doesn't believe that."

"Do I? Because he accused me of doing just that to my face."

"He was worried about Alpin. We all are, and you need to remember that."

"I'm worried about Alpin, too, but I didn't accuse anyone of hurting him." Especially after what had happened between him and Alpin back at the coven, being accused of doing something like that had been hard on Merrick.

He realized it was partly his fault that people believed he could do something like that. He hadn't been nice to Alpin in the beginning, and he'd made sure everyone knew what he thought of him. Still, there was a huge gap between being annoyed at how much Alpin talked and how he was trying to get into Merrick's pants and wanting him dead.

"I'm sure Arlen is right," Kieran said, clearly trying to soothe Merrick. "Emotions were running high, and Tyrian was worried about his son. I think you should give him the benefit of the doubt."

"As if he'll give it to me," Merrick muttered. He cleared his throat, realizing how much of a sullen teenager he sounded like. "What can I do for you? Do you know who those wolves were?"

Kieran grimaced. "I do. I recognized them, which is how I can tell you they were part of the pack once."

"Yet they attacked."

"I'm not sure why. They left when my father and sister did, and I didn't think I'd see any of them again. They were convinced I wouldn't be good for the pack, and maybe they weren't wrong."

"Or maybe they were absolutely wrong. You're doing a good job." Merrick truly believed that.

"Thank you." Kieran flopped onto the couch. He looked exhausted, and he probably was.

Merrick was tired, too, but he wouldn't rest easily until he saw Alpin.

Could he even go to sleep if he tried right now? He suspected the answer would be no. He was used to sleeping on his own, but after sharing a bed with Alpin, he didn't want to have to do so again. Of course, considering Alpin's state, it would be better for him to have space for a while, but Merrick didn't care about any of that. He'd sleep on the floor next to Alpin's bed if it meant he could be sure the vampire was all right.

He couldn't believe he'd gone and fallen in love with a vampire. He didn't even *like* vampires, for fuck's sake. He was one himself, but he'd never been happy about that, not the way Alpin was. Merrick couldn't see any positives about having to drink blood and not being able to be in the sun, but none of that mattered at the moment.

"Have you tried contacting your sister to find out what happened?" Arlen asked.

"I have," Kieran responded, "but she hasn't answered."

Which was worrying, although Merrick suspected the woman had a lot, if not everything, to do with this.

Kieran got his phone out of his pocket. He dialed a number, and Merrick knew he was calling his sister. He clearly didn't expect her to answer, because his eyes widened, and Merrick could hear a woman's voice on the other side of the phone even without putting it on speaker.

"What do you want?" she snapped.

"Fay?"

"You called my number, didn't you? And it's not the first time tonight."

"I know. I'm sorry to bother you, but I was worried."

"Why would you be worried?"

"We were attacked tonight."

There was a moment of silence. "I know."

Kieran looked stricken, as if he'd hoped his sister wouldn't have had anything to do with the attack. It was clear she was involved, though. "What do you mean, you know?"

"Who do you think sent those wolves? Did you kill all of them? How many did *they* kill?"

"They're all gone. What are you doing? Why are you sending people who belonged to the pack to hurt us?"

"Because it's the only thing to do. You're killing the pack, and I'm trying to help it."

The woman was delusional. Merrick wished he weren't listening to this conversation and wondered if he could sneak out without Arlen noticing. Kieran probably wouldn't because he was so focused on his sister.

"By killing former members?" Kieran sounded bewildered.

"I'm not the one who killed them. You are. But you'll see, Kieran. Dad and I will be back, and you'll regret everything you've done. We're not alone anymore."

Merrick's stomach turned to lead. What did she mean by that? He and Arlen looked at each other, and he could see in his best friend's eyes that Arlen was thinking the same.

Kieran clearly was, too. "Who are you talking about?" he asked softly. "Please tell me you didn't go to the dragons."

"The clan is strong, and they'll help me get the pack back. We'll kill all the bloodsuckers, and you'll regret ever opening the pack to them. You'll regret *everything*, Kieran."

Merrick didn't like any of this. Fay and the rest of the people who'd left with her had intimate knowledge of the pack. They could tell the clan a lot of things the clan normally wouldn't have found out, which would put the pack in danger.

But the pack was already in danger. The attack had exposed that, and they were about to have to learn to deal with the consequences of going against the clan.

This time, when Alpin woke up, Tyrian was sitting on a chair by his bed. He was reading a book with a black cover, but Alpin didn't get to see what it was before Tyrian noticed his eyes were open and put it away.

"How are you feeling?" Tyrian asked as he leaned closer.

Alpin took a moment to take stock of his body. He was still in pain, mostly in his neck, but he felt better than he had before. The sleep had done him good. "I feel fine. How long was I asleep?"

"It's almost dawn."

Alpin had expected Tyrian to tell him he'd been here for at least a few days, but he was glad that wasn't so. He tried sitting up and managed almost entirely on his own this time. Tyrian had to help him slide a pillow behind his back, but that was all. He fussed over Alpin until Alpin found himself smiling. What would he do without his father? He didn't know and hoped he'd never have to find out.

Alpin had lost a lot in his life. His parents had died when he was a teenager, and he'd been left to live alone in the streets. He'd had people, mostly kids around his age trying to survive, but he'd never had a family until he met Tyrian and the others. He considered them his family of the heart, and that was enough for him. He didn't need to be related to them to love them.

He looked around the room. The curtains were drawn, which made sense if the sun was rising. The tumbler was gone from the nightstand, but he knew that if he needed more blood, Tyrian would provide it.

The only thing missing was Merrick, and it hurt not to see him. It probably shouldn't, but Alpin couldn't help how he felt.

He'd thought he'd never fall in love, which in hindsight had been stupid. He was a vampire and had hundreds of years of life in front of him. Of course he was going to fall in love eventually. He hadn't expected it to happen so soon, but it didn't have to be a bad thing. It probably wasn't, but without Merrick here, it was impossible for Alpin to know.

He cleared his throat. "Where's Merrick?"

Tyrian's expression did an interesting thing, a grimace almost appearing before he smoothed it out. He looked away, but Alpin already knew he was hiding something.

He prayed it wasn't that Merrick had been hurt, too, or that he'd died.

"He's fine," Tyrian eventually said.

"You already said that, but if he's really fine, he'd be here." Right?

"He went home after bringing you back. He'd shifted, so he needed to shower, rest, and get dressed. I know Kieran wanted to talk to him, which is probably what they're doing right now."

That made sense. If Merrick had barged out of the forest in his dragon form, he'd need new clothes unless he wanted to flash everyone, and he wasn't that kind of guy. How long did it take to grab a change of clothes, though? Okay, so maybe he was talking to Kieran, but it hadn't been that late when Merrick and Alpin had arrived back in pack territory, and the night was almost over. It had been hours. Surely Merrick didn't have a good reason to stay away from Alpin now.

And Alpin was convinced Tyrian was hiding something. It was obvious from the way his father couldn't seem to look at him, and while Alpin usually wouldn't push, he didn't think he could stop himself from doing it this time. He needed to know what had happened.

"Did he do something?" That was Alpin's fear. Maybe Merrick told Tyrian that he didn't want to be with Alpin after all. Maybe he'd explained it was too much and that he was leaving Alpin in Tyrian's capable hands and never coming back. Merrick was used to being on his own. He trusted very few people, and it was possible that Alpin wasn't one of those people yet. The fact that they had sex might not mean anything to Merrick, no matter what it meant to Alpin.

"He's fine," Tyrian insisted.

Alpin swallowed and tried to move, but his throat reminded him that he wasn't going anywhere for now. "Just tell me," he begged. "If he said he wants nothing to do with me, I'll deal with it. I just need to know."

Tyrian looked conflicted. Alpin gave him his best puppy eyes, which he wasn't sure would work in his state. He was relieved to see it did when Tyrian's shoulders slumped and he leaned back in his chair.

"I sent him away."

Alpin waited for a better explanation, but it didn't come. "What do you mean you sent him away?"

"Exactly what I said. When he brought you here, I accused him of staying back and allowing the wolves to hurt you on purpose."

Alpin opened his mouth to tell Tyrian that hadn't been the case. He was outraged that Tyrian could believe something like that, but he understood where he came from. Alpin could only imagine what state he'd been in when Merrick had brought him home, and Tyrian would have been terrified. Even when he was angry, he never lashed out, but maybe he did when he was scared.

Tyrian raised a hand, stopping Alpin from saying whatever he'd been about to blurt out. He wasn't sure, to be honest.

"I realize I was wrong to say those things to him. He's an ally, and I don't actually think he would have allowed anyone to hurt you if he could have stopped it."

"I *know* he wouldn't have."

"I just needed to get to you and make sure you survived. He wanted to stay, but I told him to go home. He hasn't been back since, but Mallory mentioned that Arlen was keeping him at their house."

Which meant Merrick was probably grumpy. God, Alpin would do pretty much anything to be able to see that. "I want him here."

"I understand, but I don't think it's a good idea. It's why I sent him away. I know you've been teasing him and trying to get to him, but now isn't the right moment to continue doing so."

"I'm aware. I wouldn't want a random hookup here, but that's not what he is. I'm falling in love with him."

Tyrian's eyes widened. "Are you sure?"

"I guess. I've never been in love, so I'm not sure how it feels, but I know I don't want to be away from him. I want him here by my side while I heal."

Tyrian got to his feet. "I'm not letting anyone in, not even your siblings. You need rest, and you won't get that if people keep coming in and out of this bedroom."

"It wouldn't be people. It would only be him."

"I'm sorry, Alpin, but no, at least not for now. You can see him when you're strong enough to get out of bed and go to him."

Alpin sucked in a breath, and dammit, it hurt. "You turned me, and I consider you my father, but I'm an adult. I was an adult before you turned me, and that hasn't changed. I can make my own decisions, and my decision in this situation is that I want Merrick with me." Alpin tried to sound like he knew what he was doing, but his stomach churned at the thought of going against Tyrian's will. He didn't do things like that.

Tyrian crossed his arms over his chest. "I'm not trying to make decisions for you."

"What? That's *exactly* what you're doing."

"As your *doctor*. You need rest, more blood, and time. You don't need people bothering you."

"But he wouldn't be bothering me. I want him here."

"It'll have to wait."

Alpin could see he wouldn't change Tyrian's mind. He was kind of angry, but he didn't tell Tyrian that. They'd have to talk about this later. As much as Alpin hated to admit it, Tyrian wasn't wrong. He did need rest, and he was already sleepy again. Hopefully, the next time he woke up, he'd be able to get out of bed and go to Merrick. It was clear that Tyrian would keep him away until then, so if Alpin wanted his daily Merrick fix, he'd have to go get it himself.

CHAPTER SIX

M errick felt weird.

It had nothing to do with the fight with the wolves a few days ago or with the entire situation with the dragons. No, he felt weird because he missed Alpin and had no idea how to deal with that.

In the beginning, he hadn't even realized that was what he felt. He'd tried going to Alpin again, sneaking out of the house when Mallory had come back and distracted Arlen. Tyrian had opened the door and told Merrick to fuck off.

Well, he hadn't used those words, but he might as well have. Merrick had known there would be no convincing him to let him in, so he'd left.

He'd tried yesterday, too. Tyrian had seemed pissed to see him, and once again, he'd told him to get lost. He'd explained that Alpin was recovering and that he didn't need distractions, and while Merrick agreed with that, he'd pointed out he wasn't a distraction. He was the man Alpin loved, and surely, if Alpin was conscious, he'd have told Tyrian that. Tyrian had insisted that Alpin was all right and that he'd woken up several times, but he wouldn't tell Merrick anything else, and it was starting to worry him.

Then there was the fact that he felt as if he couldn't breathe right without Alpin by his side.

When had the man becomes essential to Merrick's happiness? It didn't make sense, especially considering they didn't know each other that well. Yet Merrick had been pacing through the house, trying to pass the time and hoping Alpin was healing quickly so he could break out and come find him.

Surely Tyrian wouldn't forbid Alpin to be with Merrick. Alpin was an adult, and while Merrick understood he loved Tyrian and respected him, it didn't give Tyrian the right to make decisions in their situation. Alpin wasn't a teenager with a crush. He was an adult man, an adult *vampire*, a predator who could kill people and drink blood. He didn't need anyone's permission to be with Merrick.

Yet Tyrian was effectively keeping them apart.

Merrick growled and glared out the window. No matter how confused he was about all of this, he was done denying his feelings. He couldn't afford to continue, and he didn't want to. He'd almost lost Alpin. It was too easy to imagine him dying, and Merrick knew how lucky he was. He could have lost Alpin and whatever future they could have together, and he wasn't willing to deal with a life without Alpin any longer than he already had. These few days had been hard enough. Somewhere down the line, Alpin had become a vital part of Merrick's life, and it hurt not to have him close.

It didn't matter that none of this made sense. The only thing that did matter was that this was how Merrick felt, and there would be no changing it.

He paced the length of the living room again. He'd been pushing everyone away for so long that he wasn't sure how to welcome someone into his life. Arlen had always been there, it seemed, as had Harmon. Mallory was new, but he wasn't really part of Merrick's life, so he and Merrick didn't spend that much time together.

Alpin was different. He was all Merrick's, at least if Merrick found the courage to tell him how much he wanted him. They had yet to talk about the time they'd spent together at the coven, and it felt almost as though if they didn't, they'd lose everything. Merrick wasn't ready for that to happen.

So this was Merrick's plan. He'd give Alpin a few days,

mostly because he was probably unconscious and didn't even know Merrick wasn't there with him. It shouldn't take much longer than that for the vampire to heal. Merrick would let Alpin come to him, and if he didn't, he'd go to the house again. If Tyrian still didn't let him in, he'd climb the side of the house and slip in. If even that didn't work, he was ready to shift into his dragon form and land on the roof, then peek into every window to try to find Alpin.

Merrick was stubborn, as was his dragon when he wanted something, and they both wanted Alpin.

But in the meantime, he couldn't stay here and continue pacing the house. He felt like he was going nuts, which meant he needed more time outside. Maybe he could shift and fly around, or even better, go patrol the area he and Alpin were responsible for. Kieran had told him it didn't matter, but Merrick felt they shouldn't risk it, especially with Alpin out of commission. For now, both the dragons and the other wolves had stayed away since the fight, but he wouldn't bet on them doing so for much longer. At least he wouldn't be distracted by Alpin, which could only be a good thing, and he'd be able to focus on the forest and on making sure no one tried sneaking in.

Decision made, he moved toward the entrance. Mallory appeared as if out of thin air, stepping in front of him. "Where are you going?"

Merrick sucked in a breath. He couldn't make an enemy out of Mallory and didn't want to. Mallory made Arlen happy, which was all Merrick wanted for his friend. "Outside."

"I can see that. I meant, where are you going precisely?"

Merrick glared. "What? Do I have to tell you when I go to the bathroom, too? I'm not going to try to see Alpin."

Mallory's shoulders relaxed. "Good."

"You agree with this bullshit? You know me. I'd never

have done anything to hurt Alpin. Even if I didn't like him, and I do, he's still an ally and your brother. I'm not that much of an asshole."

Mallory grimaced. "I never believed you'd done anything to hurt Alpin. I don't think Tyrian did, either. It's just that he's closer to Alpin than to the rest of us. I think he sees Alpin as the baby of the family, and in a way, he is. He's the youngest, and that will never change."

Since they were vampires, it definitely wouldn't.

"Anyway, he's worried about Alpin," Mallory continued, "He's not making rational decisions. We all tried talking to him. Hell, Alpin told him he hated him and that he'd never talk to him again if he didn't allow you to come, but it hasn't been enough to change Tyrian's mind. I don't think anything can."

Merrick blinked. "Alpin said that?"

"Yes. He clearly cares about you, and we all suspect something happened between the two of you."

Mallory wasn't fishing for information, but he obviously knew something had happened. Had Tyrian said something? Even though Merrick hadn't gone into details, he'd told Tyrian that he was falling in love with Alpin.

Mallory grinned. "Anyway, Tyrian knows we all disagree with his decision, but he won't change his mind. It's better to wait until Alpin's able to leave his room and come to you. Tyrian will get over this eventually, but it's better not to push him too far at the moment."

Merrick tried to relax. "I promise I'm not going there. I realized what you just said a while ago, and I decided it would be best to let Alpin come to me. I can't continue staying in the house, though. I'm going nuts with nothing to do, so I thought I'd go to the area where Alpin and I are supposed to patrol and walk around for a bit."

"You want company?"

Merrick shook his head. "You know me. I'd rather be alone."

"I do know that, and it's fine, but remember you're not alone, all right? You have Arlen and me and the rest of my family. Well, except Tyrian, at least for now."

Merrick chuckled. "I know all of that, but thanks for reminding me." Arlen would never let him forget that he wasn't alone in the world. Even if Merrick tried shutting him out, he'd find his way back in, possibly through the back window.

No, Merrick just needed some time, not being permanently left alone. He got that when he left the house and walked deep into the forest. He went back to the area he and Alpin had been patrolling, expecting to see blood, but there was nothing. All signs of the fight were gone, which was kind of eerie. It was better that way, though. Merrick didn't want a reminder of what happened to Alpin.

He started walking up and down between two imaginary spots. He knew he should be more focused, but he doubted anyone would attack so soon after losing three wolves. No matter what Kieran's sister said and believed, the clan wouldn't sacrifice dragons when they could sacrifice wolves.

A branch cracked somewhere behind Merrick, and he paused. He stood there, listening, grinning a bit when he heard someone behind him. It was only one person, which meant he could take them easily. Maybe, if he was lucky, he'd manage to get them to Kieran in one piece, and they'd give the pack details about the clan and what they were planning.

When the person behind Merrick stepped even closer, he twirled around, his hand shooting out. The figure ducked so Merrick didn't see them in the face, and he missed the throat. That was fine with him. He grabbed the man's shoulder and pulled him forward, then sideways, and slammed the man's back against the closest tree.

He was about to have fun.

Alpin wasn't exactly in the best of shape yet, so he could have done without being slammed against a tree. He whimpered, but he knew better than to try to get out of Merrick's hold before Merrick recognized him. Instead of attempting to push Merrick away, Alpin wrapped his fingers around Merrick's wrists and squeezed, hoping the gesture would be strange enough from an enemy to give Merrick pause.

That, and seeing Alpin in front of him.

Unless Merrick had intended to slam Alpin, of all people, against a tree. Alpin hoped that wasn't the case. After everything that had happened, surely Merrick was over his need to strangle Alpin.

Merrick's eyes widened and he took a step back, letting go of Alpin. Alpin didn't let go of him, though, and kept his hold on Merrick's wrists. He was afraid Merrick would run if he didn't.

"What are you doing here?" Merrick asked, pulling.

Alpin pulled back. "I wanted to see you. I missed you. I was kind of pissed you weren't there when I woke up, but Tyrian told me what he did, so I'm not angry at you anymore."

Merrick shook his head. "You should be in bed, resting, not walking around in the middle of the night."

Alpin arched a brow. "When should I be walking around, then? Certainly not in the middle of the day. It would be a bit uncomfortable."

Merrick glared, and Alpin felt better seeing that expression. He'd missed all of Merrick, even his glares—maybe especially those.

"You know what I mean. You almost died. You would have, if Tyrian hadn't given you so much blood. You should be in bed, resting, not trampling around the forest and letting me slam you against a tree."

Merrick tried moving away again, and this time, Alpin let him. He'd hoped their reunion would be like in the movies, maybe that they'd end up having sex against a tree, but he could see he'd been wrong. Merrick was freaking out, which meant Alpin was going to have to waste time reassuring him.

He wouldn't have done it for anyone else, but for Merrick, he gladly would. It was one of the reasons he knew he'd done the stupid thing and had fallen in love with Merrick. No one else could have managed to get him to feel this way.

"I've had enough of bed rest," he explained. "And before you say anything, Tyrian wasn't happy about this, but he agreed I was well enough to take a walk in the forest. Of course, he didn't know you were going to slam me against a tree, but what he doesn't know doesn't hurt him, right?"

Merrick rubbed his face. He looked tired, which would make sense. He'd probably been freaking out about Alpin and whether or not he'd survive and maybe whether or not Alpin would want him after all of this. Alpin certainly had, and he wasn't quite sure how to deal with it yet.

"Well, whatever Tyrian said, you should go home. You look tired." Merrick's expression was uncompromising.

"And here I thought I looked beautiful." Alpin had seen his reflection in the mirror before leaving the house, so he knew Merrick was right. He looked like a wolf shifter had used him as a chew toy and spit him up once they were done, and it wasn't that far from the truth.

"You always look beautiful, but you're not fully healed yet. Let's go. I'm taking you home."

Alpin went along with it because he knew Merrick needed to feel like he was protecting him, but part of him was anxious. So far, the only thing Merrick had talked about was that Alpin should still be resting in bed. Had he changed his mind?

Or maybe he'd always felt like they shouldn't be together. They hadn't talked much about the time they'd spent together at the coven, but Alpin had believed they had time to do it. He hadn't wanted to rush Merrick into things, especially when it had been obvious Merrick was uncomfortable. He hadn't expected they'd be attacked, but they had, and it had changed things. Alpin hadn't known where he stood before, and it hadn't gotten better. Unfortunately, the only way to know would be to ask and talk about how he and Merrick felt, and it wasn't something he was used to.

He liked that Merrick wrapped a protective arm around his waist, though. He was giving Alpin the option of leaning against him if he needed help walking, and at the same time, he was keeping them close. If he'd been afraid that Alpin might die, it would make sense that he wanted him close now, right? He wanted to reassure himself that Alpin was all right.

So Alpin took advantage of that and allowed Merrick to guide him through the forest and back toward the cluster of houses where many of the pack shifters lived. Alpin could have done without the second trek through the forest, but he wasn't alone anymore, which was what he'd been aiming for.

"I really thought you'd visit me," he gently teased as they walked.

Merrick didn't look at him, but Alpin suspected he'd glare if he did.

"You told me Tyrian explained what happened," Merrick said.

"He did, but you could have climbed in through the window or something."

Merrick turned to stare at Alpin. "Is that something you'd have wanted me to do?"

Alpin shrugged, then instantly regretted it because, damn, it hurt. "I don't know. I guess it would have been nice not to be on my own. Tyrian didn't even allow my siblings to visit.

He said I needed rest."

"He wasn't wrong. You didn't see yourself after you were wounded, but Tyrian and I both did. It was terrifying. The wound on your throat, the blood you lost, and how pale you were—it was all horrible. You can't blame your father for freaking out."

Alpin sighed. "I don't blame him for that. Hell, I understand why he did. I *do* blame him for making decisions for me when I was perfectly capable of doing so."

"You were unconscious when I took you home."

"Yeah, but I didn't *stay* unconscious. It took me a few tries, but I was fine after Tyrian got enough blood into me." Merrick looked skeptical, so Alpin added, "In pain, but fine. I told him I wanted to see you, and he said he'd forbidden you to visit. Before he admitted that, I thought you'd decided I wasn't worth hanging around and waiting for me to heal, and it hurt almost as much as the wound on my throat." Alpin reached up to touch the bandages that were still present there.

He'd always have the scars. There was no way around that, but he didn't really care. The scars would be proof of how strong he was and what he'd survived, and they wouldn't take anything away from him. He was pretty sure Merrick would find him sexy even with scars, because after all, he found Merrick sexy with his scars.

"You wanted me there?" Merrick asked, sounding strangely vulnerable.

Alpin stopped walking and pulled Merrick back. Merrick carefully avoided looking at him, but Alpin didn't care. If Merrick didn't want what he was offering, he'd tell him and push him away. He'd never been shy about any of this.

But when Alpin kissed him, Merrick didn't push him away. Instead, he wrapped his arms around Alpin as if he were fragile, and maybe he was. Merrick held him close, kissing him back so gently it made Alpin want to cry.

He'd never expected anything like this to happen, but he was glad it had. He didn't want anyone but Merrick, and it looked like he wasn't the only one who felt that way.

"You need more rest," Merrick murmured against Alpin's lips.

"I won't say I don't." Alpin was pretty tired, and he suspected Tyrian would get more blood into him before allowing him to go back to bed. He'd also make sure to tell Alpin that he'd told him so, but Alpin didn't care. He was exhausted, but he needed to do this. He needed time with Merrick and for them to talk and finally clear things up. He wouldn't rest easily until he knew where they stood and what Merrick expected from him.

"Let me take you home," Merrick said.

"I'll let you take me home, but not right away. I spent too much time in that bed and need some fresh air."

Merrick didn't look convinced, but he still nodded. Alpin almost couldn't believe it. Merrick really would give him anything he asked for, wouldn't he? He wanted Alpin to be happy, just like Alpin wanted him to be happy.

It *definitely* was time to talk.

Merrick wanted nothing more than to bundle Alpin off and rush him back into bed, but he understood where Alpin was coming from. Since the fight, he'd been stuck in a bed, away from everyone. It had only been a few days, and most people would have been okay with that, but not him. Alpin was a social creature. He needed more than four walls and his father to keep him company.

So when Alpin said he wanted more time before he went back to bed, Merrick took his hand and held it as they strolled between the trees, avoiding the houses for the moment. It was slow going, but Merrick wasn't in a rush.

They were silent, and things between them were both easy and tense. Merrick wasn't sure what to do or say, and maybe he was a coward, but it was easier to let Alpin take the first step. He had no doubt Alpin would eventually, and he grinned in the darkness when Alpin started talking.

He'd been right.

"We should have talked before driving back," Alpin said. "It would have made things less awkward. It certainly would have helped when I thought you'd abandoned me."

Merrick hated that Alpin had felt that, but it wasn't his fault. He might understand why Tyrian had told him to stay away, but it didn't mean he agreed with what the vampire had done. Alpin had been hurt, and keeping him from the people who cared the most about him wasn't right.

"So here goes," Alpin said, sucking in a breath. "I didn't even know it was possible for me to feel this way, but I've fallen in love with you."

Merrick had known that, yet the words were enough to make him breathless.

Alpin didn't seem to realize what was happening and continued talking. "I have no idea when it happened, but as it is, I want nothing more than to spend time with you. I realize you have work to do at the club and to protect the pack, and I won't demand that you spend all your free time with me or tell me that you have feelings for me, but I'd be grateful if you could give me a chance. I know you didn't like me in the beginning, and I won't push you because I don't want to make you angry, but this isn't just flirting for me. That morning at the coven wasn't just sex."

Alpin was already putting his hands forward in case Merrick rejected him.

Merrick couldn't blame him after the way he'd behaved when it came to Alpin initially, and he hated himself for what he'd done. That was him, though. He pushed people away, especially exuberant vampires who wanted nothing more than to get into his pants. He'd known since day one that Alpin would disrupt his life, and he'd been right.

But he couldn't find it in himself to regret it.

This time, he was the one who stopped walking. Alpin stopped instantly, already so very much attuned to Merrick. Alpin blinked, probably waiting for Merrick to explain what was happening. Merrick wasn't quite sure himself, but he owed it to Alpin, to be honest. He owed it to himself, even though it felt like the hardest thing he'd ever done. Never mind the clan and the fight coming for them. *This* was the moment Merrick was most afraid of.

He still barreled forward. "It wasn't just sex for me, either. I don't know how it's possible with how annoying you are, but I've fallen in love with you."

The words tasted weird on Merrick's tongue, but he couldn't take them back, and he didn't want to. Alpin deserved to hear them, and more importantly, he *needed* to hear them. He was clearly hesitant and off-balance after what happened to him with the wolves, and Merrick didn't blame him. It had been terrifying for him, and he hadn't even been the one wounded.

Alpin peered at him. "Really?"

"Would I lie about something like that?"

Alpin frowned. "Maybe to me, although you'd do it to try to keep me away, so maybe telling me you're in love with me isn't the best idea."

Merrick shook his head. He was pretty sure Alpin was teasing, but just in case, he wanted things to be clear between them. He'd been hesitant in the beginning, but now, he knew how he felt and what he wanted. There was no hesitation anymore, at least not on his part.

He cupped Alpin's cheek, smiling when Alpin instantly looked up at him. "These are the scariest words I've ever said, but I love you. I never thought I'd be able to open myself to another vampire after what happened with the man who turned me. Harmon is the only vampire I've ever trusted, but now, there's you, too. You're special. You didn't take my growls and snobbishness seriously, and you pushed your way under my shell. You made sure I knew you cared about me and that I couldn't live without you."

Alpin laughed. "I didn't realize I cared about you until recently, but I'm glad you trust me. It makes me feel special."

"Because you are. I'm sure you've guessed that my maker forcibly turned me into a vampire. I'm not the only one he did that to. Harmon was in the same position, which is the main reason we became close. I trust him with my life, just like I trust Arlen and you. You've become part of a very small circle of people I consider family."

Alpin grinned. "As long as you don't consider me your brother like you do Arlen and Harmon, I'm fine with it."

Merrick wasn't sure what he'd do with Alpin, but for the first time, he allowed himself to be excited about this. Whatever happened next, it sounded like he and Alpin would face it together, and there was nothing he wanted more.

The future was terrifying. The clan wasn't going anywhere until they got what they wanted, which was for the pack to be gone from the surface of the earth. Even though Merrick didn't fully trust anyone but the three people he'd mentioned just now, he liked Kieran, his people, and Alpin's family. He'd defend them because of that and because it was the right thing to do. The clan couldn't be allowed to take control of the supernatural world. That way lay madness and disaster, and Merrick wasn't ready for the world to be burned down.

"So we're doing this?" Alpin asked.

There was excitement in his tone, as well as fear, and Merrick understood and shared both those feelings. They were doing something new, but they were doing it together. No matter what Merrick had or hadn't expected, he wanted everything Alpin was ready to give him.

He nodded and kissed Alpin's forehead. "I guess we are."

"Everyone's going to freak out." Alpin sounded positively gleeful.

Merrick shook his head, but he was smiling. "You're going to get me into so much trouble."

Alpin wrapped his arms around Merrick's neck and pulled him close, pressing their foreheads together. "Maybe, but aren't I the best kind of trouble?"

Merrick pulled him close. "You are, and I wouldn't want it any other way. So you want me?"

Alpin rolled his eyes. "I'm not sure how else I could tell you that I do. Do you want me to strip naked here?"

"Better not. You're not completely healed yet."

"Then maybe I could slap some sense into you. Yes, I want you. I want you in my life and in my bed. Whatever happens next, I want us to face it together. We'll give the clan hell, and we'll settle down here in town once we're done dealing with them. I'll be close to my brother, and you and Arlen will rebuild the club. I'm not sure what I'll do for a living, but I'm rich, so that won't be a problem."

Merrick found himself smiling. He's never thought he could smile so much, and maybe he hadn't been able to before. Maybe he'd needed Alpin to show him how to do it. "You're rich, huh?"

"Yep. You can be a house husband if you want."

Merrick couldn't imagine himself staying at home that way, but he supposed it was nice not to have too much pressure to rebuild the club and have it go as well as it had before. Besides, if they started rebuilding now, he suspected the clan would just burn it down again.

But no matter what happened with the club and the clan, Merrick was happy, and that wasn't something the clan could take away from him.

Alpin was smiling so hard that his cheeks hurt. It wasn't just because Merrick had told him he wanted him. It was everything that had just happened, from what Merrick had said about how he became a vampire to him apparently agreeing to rely on Alpin when it came to the club and surviving. Alpin wanted to tell him that everything he had was Merrick's, but he knew better than to do that. Some things would take time, and he was fine with that.

After a moment, Merrick gently pushed him away. He clearly wanted to get Alpin back home, and Alpin agreed. He was kind of tired, and he couldn't wait to sit down. He didn't want to be away from Merrick, though, so he grabbed Merrick's hand as they started walking again, as much for support as because he just wanted Merrick close.

"So, we're dating," he declared.

Merrick seemed amused. "Is that all you got from the conversation we just had?"

"Not all, but that's the most important thing, isn't it? You're my boyfriend."

Merrick snorted. "I'm not sure I'd call you my boyfriend. What I feel for you is much stronger than a love story between two teenagers."

"Well, I'm not calling you my lover. I'm not ninety years old."

Merrick arched a brow. "Really? How old are you, then?"

Alpin waved Merrick's words away. "None of your business."

"I thought it was, since I'm your boyfriend."

Oh, Alpin liked this side of Merrick. He hadn't met it before, but now that he had, he hoped to see it often. It was nice to see Merrick relaxed and able to joke with him. He knew how precious this was. Merrick didn't allow himself to be like this with many people. Actually, he probably only allowed himself to be like this with three people, and one of those people was Alpin.

Alpin sighed in happiness. He didn't know what he'd done to deserve all of this, but he'd do everything he could not to lose it. Now that he had his claws in Merrick, he wasn't letting go.

Alpin swung their linked hands as they walked. "So, are you taking me home?"

"It would be the smartest thing to do. I'm sure that if I don't take you there, Tyrian will come looking for me. He might even threaten me like he did the other day."

"Did you growl at him?"

Merrick flashed Alpin his fangs. "Of course I did. What kind of boyfriend would I be if I didn't threaten your father?"

Alpin laughed. "Indeed. Well, you can threaten him as much as you want. Sometimes, he can be an asshole. I made sure he knew how I felt about him doing what he did, and I don't think he'll do it again, but just in case, maybe it's not the best idea to go home with you on my heels. Especially since I have no intention of letting you go anytime soon." Alpin wiggled his eyebrows so Merrick would know what he was talking about.

Merrick shook his head. "We're not having sex right now."

Alpin pouted. "Why not?"

"You lost a massive amount of blood, and you're still wounded. It's a miracle you can walk around, let alone trek in the forest. Tyrian might have been harsh and a bit of a dickhead, but he only did it because he cares about you. If we want him to accept me, we have to keep him happy, and that includes not hurting you again."

"But I don't have sex with my throat."

Merrick's eyes widened.

Alpin laughed. "Okay, sometimes, I do have sex with my throat. I don't need my throat if you fuck me, though. My ass didn't get hurt."

Merrick shook his head. "You're going to keep me on my toes."

"I will, and you love it."

Merrick raised Alpin's hand and kissed the back of it. "I suspect I will."

Alpin almost swooned, but he wasn't sure if it was because of Merrick or because he felt a bit weak. For all that he was eager about having sex, he was pretty sure Merrick was right and that he needed more rest.

But that didn't mean he needed to get that rest in his bed back at the house he shared with his family.

"How about I call Tyrian and tell him that I'm not coming home right now, but also promise I'll get some rest?" he offered. "I can sleep in your bed as well as I can sleep in mine." He'd actually sleep better there, but he felt a bit too exposed to be honest about that.

He'd already told Merrick so many things he'd never told anyone that one more thing probably wouldn't change much, but Alpin needed to keep himself protected for just a bit longer.

Thankfully, Merrick nodded after thinking for a moment. "You can sleep in my bed."

Alpin tried his best not to look like an overeager child as he beamed. "Great."

They walked in silence for a while, but Alpin had never been great at keeping his mouth shut. He was glad he and Merrick had talked and that they decided they were dating, but now, he had many more questions.

"So, how does dating work?" he asked.

Merrick chuckled. "I knew you wouldn't be able to stay quiet for long."

"You also knew what you were getting into when you decided to date me."

"That much is true. Haven't you ever dated anyone?"

Alpin almost shrugged, then remembered how much it hurt to do that. "Not really. Back when I was human, it would have been too dangerous. After I was turned into a vampire, I decided to have fun."

"Well, we don't have to do anything weird, especially since you're still healing. We can spend time together, getting to know each other. It's mostly talking."

"But not only, right? Because I want more sex."

Merrick laughed again.

It was good to hear him like this. It made Alpin feel ten feet tall, and he was ready to do pretty much anything to make Merrick laugh again.

"We'll have more sex," Merrick readily agreed. "Once you're healed. For now, let me take care of you, all right? We'll go home, I'll check if there's some blood in the fridge and get it ready for you, and we can snuggle in bed and maybe watch something. It's been forever since I allowed myself to waste time watching a movie."

Alpin could see that. Merrick was focused, and with everything with the clan, it made sense that he hadn't allowed himself to relax. "What about the future?" he asked. He hadn't missed the fact that Merrick had offered to warm up some blood for him when he usually refused to even come into contact with it.

That was how much Merrick cared about him.

Merrick hesitated. "We don't know what's going to happen with the clan, so I don't want to make promises I might not be able to keep."

"I think I need to hear promises, though." It made Alpin feel vulnerable, but this was Merrick.

"Well, I *can* promise you I'll do everything I can to be there for you. I'll protect you and try my best to make you happy. Hopefully, I'll be able to do that for decades to come."

That was more than Alpin had expected and almost more than Merrick could promise. There was no way for them to know what would happen with the clan, but Alpin had every intention of coming out of this fight alive, dragging Merrick with him if he had to.

Alpin was positive everything would be all right. It had to be. He couldn't even think about a world in which Merrick wouldn't be in it, which meant it wouldn't happen.

He'd make sure of it.

They fell silent again, for which Alpin was glad, because he was having a hard time not panting. He didn't want Merrick to see how tired he was, but he had no doubt Merrick knew. He held him closer as they neared the house, and Alpin readily allowed Merrick to hold most of his weight. He was relieved when they finally climbed the porch steps, but Merrick had to pick him up and carry him inside because his legs weren't cooperating. That caused a bit of alarm from Mallory and Arlen, but both Merrick and Alpin were quick to reassure them.

Alpin was perfectly fine, even though he was tired, hungry, and in some pain. He was in Merrick's arms, though, and in the end, that was all that mattered to him.

CHAPTER SEVEN

"There's a fire in town," Kieran said, immediately getting Merrick's attention.

Merrick got to his feet, the phone still by his ear. "Arlen and I will be there as soon as we can," he promised.

"I'm headed there, too."

"Be careful."

"You, too."

Merrick hung up and looked at Arlen. The two of them had been eating dinner while Mallory and Alpin spent time with their family, and they left everything as it was on the table. They'd have time to clean up later. For now, they needed to focus on the fire.

Merrick's mouth tasted bitter. This was too close to the fire at the club, and he wished he didn't have to think about that. Someone was losing their business, something they'd built over the years, and it was devastating. Merrick knew exactly how that felt. Anything he could do to help, he'd do without hesitating.

He quickly texted Alpin as he and Arlen went so his boyfriend would know what was happening, and he wasn't surprised to find out Alpin was already aware of the fire.

We got a call, too, Alpin texted back. *We're headed there right now.*

It was terrifying. Alpin had healed, but Merrick was still afraid he'd get hurt again. He'd tried convincing Alpin to stay out of the fight with the clan, but Alpin had told him to fuck off without even pausing to think about it. Merrick hadn't actually expected Alpin to say yes, so he hadn't been surprised, but he was freaking out.

"It's scary," Arlen murmured as he drove.

"You think Mallory went, too?"

"I'm sure of it. You're texting with Alpin, right? And he's going."

"How do you know?"

"Your expression. You look pissed and terrified at the same time, and Alpin's the only person who can make you look that way. I get it, but we can't forbid them to do what they need to do, and we can't live in fear."

"But Mallory was an enforcer. He's been trained to do this, while Alpin hasn't."

"Maybe not, but it doesn't mean he doesn't know what he's doing. Tyrian trained all of them so they could defend themselves if they had to."

But there was no defending anything from a fire. Hopefully, no one would throw themselves inside before Arlen and Merrick got there. As dragons, they had a certain immunity to fire, an immunity their vampire boyfriends didn't have.

Merrick stayed tense all the way to town, which, thankfully, wasn't far. They didn't have to ask where the fire was. They could see the light from afar, and Arlen headed straight there, parking by the sidewalk next to other cars and trucks. The fire department was already there, but the sight of a woman crying in front of the building broke Merrick's heart. He had no doubt she was the owner.

Thankfully, Alpin and his siblings, along with Kieran, were standing on the sidewalk, staring at the building with grim expressions.

"Anyone inside?" Arlen asked once they reached the group.

"We don't know. Lucy said the store was closed, so there shouldn't be anyone, but Alpin is convinced he heard a voice.

We almost had to restrain him to keep him out here."

Merrick turned his attention to Alpin, who was glaring. Sure enough, Mallory was holding on to him. "I heard someone call for help," he said.

Arlen and Merrick looked at each other. It was a possibility, no matter what the owner said. "Is it possible that someone needed a place to stay for the night and broke in?" Maybe the fire didn't have anything to do with the clan.

Kieran grimaced. "I suppose anything's possible."

"Do we know what started the fire?"

"The clan left a message."

Merrick didn't want to know what the message said. He could imagine too easily. "All right. I'll go inside and see if I can find anyone."

Alpin looked relieved, then immediately worried. "What if you get hurt?"

"I'll be fine. I'm a dragon, remember?"

"I'll go with him," Arlen said.

Merrick didn't try to change his mind. He wouldn't be able to.

They had to walk around to building since the firefighters were working in front of it. They didn't want anyone to see them sneak in, mostly so they wouldn't have to explain to anyone that they were dragons. Most humans didn't believe in the supernatural world, and most supernatural beings wanted to keep things that way. Merrick wasn't sure they'd be able to depending on what the clan was up to, but for now, he had other things to focus on.

He and Arlen paused by the back door, looked at each other, and nodded. Merrick reached for the door handle, and sure enough, it was warm. His hand would have been burned if he'd been human, but thankfully, he was a dragon. Still, he and Arlen would have to be careful. They could still get hurt, and badly.

Merrick pushed open the door and peeked in. He could see the fire on the other side of the building, with a partially collapsed wall. It didn't take him long to find the person Alpin had heard, but they were right under the wall.

"Dammit," Merrick swore as he pushed inside the building, Arlen right behind him.

They made a beeline for the figure under the collapsed wall. Merrick almost expected the person to be dead, so he was stunned when a hand reached up after he and Arlen managed to move the debris on top of them.

The man was alive.

The man was wearing all black, but part of his long-sleeved t-shirt had burned. Merrick could see the man's arms, and they were bright red and black and no doubt hurt like hell.

He and Arlen didn't hesitate. They reached for the guy at the same time and hauled him to his feet. Merrick winced at the pained sound the man made, but they couldn't leave him here, and there was no time for them to wait for someone to come help. There were plenty of people outside who would make sure he wasn't in pain as soon as possible, but first, they needed to get out of this building.

The ceiling creaked, and the heat became worse as they made their way toward the door. It was slow going, up until the point when Arlen gave in and reached down to grab the guy. The man screamed, which Merrick was pretty sure he would have, too, in his place.

They rushed outside, Arlen in the front, Merrick right behind him. He was almost out when the ceiling creaked again and came down, but thankfully, Merrick managed to throw himself forward and avoid it. He was breathing hard, but the air was fresh, and he sucked in one breath, then another.

"What's your name?" Arlen was asking as he rushed a guy around the building.

"Madison," the man croaked. "I swear, I told them I didn't

want to be involved. I wasn't okay with this. I tried to stop them, but I couldn't. I—"

Merrick and Arlen looked at each other with wide eyes. Was this guy the person who'd burned down the building? At the very least, it sounded like he'd been involved. "Who did this?" Merrick asked, even though he was pretty sure he should wait.

"Fay gave the order," Madison said, his voice growing fainter. "I never wanted to hurt anyone. I never wanted to leave the pack."

This was way above Merrick's pay grade. From what the guy had just said, Madison had been part of the pack and had left when Fay and the others who thought Kieran wasn't doing a good job had. Kieran would know him, and hopefully, he'd know what to do with him.

Because Merrick had no idea.

He and Arlen reached the group waiting for them. Kieran's eyes widened when he saw Madison, and he rushed forward, stopping before touching him. "Madison?"

Madison's eyes were wide. "I swear I didn't want to do this. That's why they left me inside to die. I tried to convince them to stop, but Fay has too much control over them."

Kieran looked lost, which Merrick could understand. *He* felt lost, and he wasn't the alpha, which meant he didn't have to be the one making decisions. This wouldn't be easy.

But then, nothing ever was when the clan was involved.

Kieran nodded. "We'll have time to talk later. For now, Merrick and Arlen will go with you to the hospital. They'll keep an eye on you until I can come and get you. I want to believe you, but I don't know if I can trust you."

Madison sobbed, but he nodded. A tear left a track in the soot on his cheek, but either he didn't notice, or he didn't care.

"I just want to come home," he whispered.

"You will," Kieran promised.

Merrick couldn't see that Kieran had other options, but he wondered—had Madison really been abandoned because he'd tried stopping the fire, or had he been placed there to infiltrate the pack and create trouble from the inside?

ABOUT THE AUTHOR

Catherine is the creator of several series, most of them paranormal, including the Whitedell Pride Series and the Gillham Pack Series. While she graduated in translation, she decided to go the writer's way because it was more fun to create her own stories and characters.

She's been living in Italy for more than twenty years, but she's a daughter of the North—Belgium to be precise—and she misses it so much that she's already planning to move back.

She loves pizza—probably too much—her son, her pets, and of course, books. She sneaks some reading time into her schedule every time she has five minutes free from writing, demands from her various pets and son, and lastly, housework.

Connect with her:

lievens.catherine@gmail.com
BookBub: https://www.bookbub.com/authors/catherine-lievens
Website: https://authorcatherinelievens.com/
Facebook: https://www.facebook.com/catherine.lievens.9
Facebook Group: https://www.facebook.com/groups/411778002341528/
Twitter: https://twitter.com/authorCLievens
Newsletter: http://eepurl.com/c-uvKn

www.ingramcontent.com/pod-product-compliance
Lightning Source LLC
Chambersburg PA
CBHW071626140626
46555CB00021B/804